Freja

Elizabeth Grey

SNOWFLAKE
PUBLISHING

Please visit www.elizabeth-grey.com **to sign up to Elizabeth Grey's newsletter and for more information on her books.**

Facebook: www.facebook.com/elizabethgreyauthor
Twitter: www.twitter.com/elizabethjgrey
Instagram: www.instagram.com/elizabethgreyauthor

Freja – When We Were Young

Published 2018
ISBN-13: 978-1718064980

Set in 12 pt, Times New Roman.

Cover designed by Elizabeth Grey Art & Illustration of South Shields, Tyne and Wear, UK.

Copy Edited by Kia Thomas Editing of South Shields, Tyne and Wear, UK.
www.kiathomasediting.com
www.twitter.com/kiathomasedits

<u>Dedicated to the voiceless</u>

<u>Acknowledgements</u>

Kia, Kara & Andrea – as always

David – cheers for the Danish swears

Alison I, Alison C & Grace – I see you and
THANKS

<u>Chris – for being super-supportive hubster and
super-dedicated Dad</u>

Content Warning

This book contains a scene of non-graphic assault
which some readers might find upsetting.

TABLE OF CONTENTS

Present Day

I slowly exhale a heavy breath full of sad memories as I make a connection between Violet's life and my own. "I found my soulmate years later, but I lost him. I let other people take him – and my dreams – away from me."

I feel my eyes glisten with unshed tears as concern creeps over my friend's beautiful face. I want to tell her everything. I want to talk to her. But I've never told anybody. It was easier to block it all out and forget.

"How? What happened?" she asks.

"It's a long and complicated story and there isn't enough time to tell you now, but I want you to understand something. I lost my soulmate for completely different reasons to why I lost Per. I thought he wasn't ready, but I realised too late that it was me who wasn't ready. I didn't know how to fight for him, so I let him go."

1

"MY AMERICAN DREAM IS DEAD."

Four pairs of drunken, partied-out eyes fall upon me as I stumble into the living room and kick off my heels. "Billy Moss is a pervert. An entitled pervert. The type of pervert who thinks he can put his roaming octopus testicles . . . I mean tentacles . . . wherever the hell he likes"

JJ, my best friend, leaps out of his chair with a wobble. "That guy had 'son of a bitch' written all over his face. He said hello to you by licking your ear, for fuck's sake – you should have known, and I shouldn't have left you alone in Sound. That place has always been a dive."

"I wasn't alone. I was with Marie and Dana. At least, I think I was . . ." Something funny is happening in my head, as if my brain is trying to shake off the alcohol fog so it can do some thinking. "Oh, wait a minute . . . *åh min Gud*! The last time I saw Dana, she was going to the bathroom but asked me to share a taxi home with her. Billy Moss's even pervier best friend wouldn't leave her alone." I rummage around in my bag for my cell phone. "Fuck! I forgot to wait for her. How could I do that?"

"Freja, relax. You know Dana is real smart. She'll be fine," says Peyton, my roomie and co-worker. She's trying to calm me down, but all I can think about is Dana and the fact I'm the shittiest friend on the planet. I check my texts. Crap, I have around fifteen of them. Why is Logan still trying to call me? I told him two weeks ago that we were over. Oh thank goodness, Dana went home with Katrina and Joe. But what the hell? How many people have I given my number to tonight? There was a guy with a tattoo and . . . oh, shit and damn, if this doesn't make me never drink again, I don't know what will. "Guys, you have to help me. I've given Howard James my cell number."

JJ and Aaron gasp in horror.

Peyton and Richie stare at me blankly.

"Who the hell is Howard James?" asks Richie. He's my sensible English friend and other roomie. I need him to do the thing he always does: scold me affectionately, then help me fix it.

"Howard has classes with us at UCLA," JJ says, shaking his head admonishingly at me. "He has a killer Freja-crush."

"He's asked me out eleven times," I say with a shudder. "It started when we invited him and his group of musical theatre majors out with us for spring break. We were in this dive bar downtown, and it was a bit of a crazy night."

"What Freja means is . . ." A huge grin crawls across JJ's face. "She stripped down to a pink bikini, morphed into Shakira and danced to 'Hips Don't Lie' on top of the bar."

I can barely remember doing it, if I'm honest, but the feedback was awesome.

I read Howard's text: *Can't wait for our date. I've been wanting to find out if your hips really don't lie since spring break.* Ugh, what the fuck does that mean? I can't even think of texting him back until I'm sober. "My life sucks. I should be dating a hot movie star; or I should be planning what to wear for this year's Oscars." I flop down on the sofa next to JJ, bringing my feet into his lap. "Why aren't I deciding between five blockbuster movie offers? How did I get here, huh? Sometime over the last two years, Uncle Sam must have bribed a bald eagle to fly over my American dream and shit on it from the greatest of heights."

Nobody responds, because everybody knows I'm right.

When I left Denmark two years ago I was fearless. I never once doubted I was going to kill it in Hollywood. I thought I'd be an overnight success, with millions of fans and every accolade the industry has to offer landing at my feet. I'd be spending my days auditioning for top movies and hit TV shows. My evenings would be split between learning lines, attending all the coolest celeb parties and collecting Best Actress awards at top ceremonies (hello, Oscar!). As for my weekends? Hot and steamy sexual encounters with Leonardo diCaprio fitted effortlessly into my plan.

But now I realise I had my head up my ass. I'm studying the tedious technicalities of film production at college instead of auditioning for movie roles. I'm working as a waitress at the Cosmic Diner instead of attending celebrity parties. And then we come to the biggest disappointment – a truth so earth-shatteringly depressing that the beers I've thrown down my neck all night can't drown it out. I'm still – tragically, shamefully –

single. Leonardo diCaprio's invitation to play Hide the Salami must have got lost in the mail. Along with my fucking Oscar.

"Looks like you need a top-up, sis." JJ picks up a jug full of pina colada and fills everyone's glasses.

"Are you ever going to stop calling me 'sis', JJ?" He pulls my feet back into his lap and tenderly rubs my leg. "Having to explain to people that we're not related is exhausting."

"So don't tell them. I don't mind. I'd love it if you were my sister."

"You do look remarkably alike," Richie chips in with a laugh.

"We do not!" I protest, even though I know there are glaringly obvious physical similarities. We're both pale, freckly and ginger, like human versions of Raggedy Ann and Andy.

"Yes, we do look alike," protests JJ. "And we also have the same taste in men."

Aaron, his partner of four years, gives me a wink and blows me a kiss.

My sozzled head is pounding, so I hold back my laugh for fear that my skull might explode. I'd go to bed with a jug of iced water and extra-strength Tylenol if I wasn't desperate for company. "I only fell for a hot gay guy once, that guest lecturer on diversity in film casting. In my defence, he was very pretty and—"

"And clearly the gayest man in the room!" shrieks JJ. "You also came on to Perry the Pianist, who, if memory serves, was wearing white plaid shorts at the time. I mean, come on. If he'd dressed up as Liberace and started singing 'I'm Too Sexy' you'd probably have still tried to bang him."

11

"Okay, okay. I admit my gaydar might be a little bit off."

"Sweetheart, it's never been on," he says with as much West Coast attitude as he can muster. "You were probably hot for me when we first met."

I think back to Orientation week at UCLA, and a terrifying memory floats into my mind, involving way too many cocktails and a really dumb idea to streak around campus. "The day we met you managed to get me naked within five hours, so maybe it was *you* who was hot for *me*."

"That escapade was all your idea, and while you had no problem with some creep in our year filming us and uploading it to Myspace, the partners at my law firm weren't overjoyed I got naked with my 'sister'." JJ shakes his head wearily at me.

Richie laughs. "Come on, JJ, you know Freja is too cool to be your sister. She's cooler than everybody."

Richie runs Santa Monica's Sunshine Community Theatre, but he wants to make it in Hollywood just as much as I do. So far, his English accent has been useful in landing him gangster bad-guy roles, but they've always been short-lived. Literally short-lived. Every single character he's played has been killed by a gun, or a knife, or an arrow or – in one TV show – a fire truck driven by an amnesiac circus clown.

"I don't think I can drink anymore, guys." Peyton places her hand on her slender hip and grimaces. "I think I've got an alcohol cramp."

"What the hell?" My voice is shrill with outrage. "There's no such thing as alcohol cramp, Peyton. Don't be a lightweight, and don't leave me to drown

12

my sorrows with these three. You've been looking forward to a childfree night for weeks."

Like me and a million other twenty-something West Coast residents, Peyton is an aspiring actress, and a very resentful waitress. Unlike me she's a blonde, blue-eyed California girl with so much Malibu Barbie DNA in her gene pool she must poo plastic. She is also a single mom whose parents are kind enough to regularly help her out with childcare. "I guess I don't feel like celebrating tonight."

Oh crap, I forgot. Why do I keep forgetting important friend-related things? Peyton split up with her surfer boyfriend – aka Malibu Ken – this morning. I'm always Peyton's go-to girl whenever she needs a shoulder to cry on, so why haven't I been called on for tissues and sympathy? They'd only been dating for two weeks, but I still should have realised Peyton would be bummed out.

I haul myself up to a sitting position and wait for the right words to come, but they don't. *Focus, Freja, Focus!* I take a deep breath, but my brain is too foggy. Oh my god, that's it! Alcohol is my kryptonite. I must have temporarily destroyed my empathic superpowers through excessive cocktail consumption.

"I'm so sorry about . . . um . . ." Fuck! Why can't I remember the guy's name? Damn you, alcohol. "I'm so sorry about your break-up."

Peyton rolls her eyes and I don't blame her. I would kick my own ass if it were physically possible. "He has a name, Freja."

"I'm sorry," I say guiltily. Ugh, I'm never drinking again. Not ever. "I . . . um . . ."

13

She raises her eyebrows. "You can't remember his name, can you?"

"Of course I can. It's . . ." *Don't say Ken, don't say Ken, don't say Ken.* "Karl. That's it. I'm sorry about Karl."

Her eyes stop rolling in order to throw daggers. "Kyle."

Damn it! "I'm sorry, I'm just too drunk to be me right now. I'll make it up to you when I've sobered up, I promise."

"This is your biggest problem, Freja. You're always drunk." The snippiness in her voice takes me by surprise. "You spent so much time ogling Kyle's biceps, it's little wonder you never bothered to learn his name."

My body stiffens in anger. I feel JJ's hand grip my knee. "What is that supposed to mean?"

Peyton glances at Aaron, whose blue eyes shift immediately to the floor. Richie nervously clears his throat. JJ's hold on my knee grows firmer, as if he's trying to hold me back. And as if by magic, the fog lifts and my superpowers return. All four of them have something they want to say to me.

"What's going on, guys?"

"Maybe we should leave this for another time," Richie says to everyone in the room but me.

"I don't want to leave it, so spill," I say to Richie, who clams up and stares at his feet.

My gaze returns to Peyton, who promptly gulps down the rest of her pina colada. Crap, is she seeking courage from a stiff drink? "Sorry, Freja. There's no easy way to say this, but it has to be said." She puts her glass down on the coffee table with a clunk. "Richie and I feel you're not pulling your weight."

Betrayal churns in my stomach like sour milk. "Oh."

"Yeah. We get you have the smallest room, but we think you should contribute more."

I look at Richie, but his eyes refuse to meet mine. "You want me to pay more rent?"

"Yes, and step up in paying the bills," she says.

I feel my eyes grow wide with shock. This is unfair. "I'm studying part-time and working at the diner most nights. I do my best."

"Your best isn't good enough," she declares. Her voice is commanding, and I wouldn't be surprised if she'd rehearsed this confrontation word for word. "I cooked for you five times this week. Sure, I enjoy cooking, but when was the last time you cooked? You never pick up after yourself, and we're tired of you treating our home like a hotel. And we're tired of the strange guys you bring back here. My daughter lives here too. I have her safety to think about."

Peyton's words drip into my brain like poison. Have I been inconsiderate? Should I have volunteered to pay more? I don't know where this has come from, but I know I haven't put Riley in danger. "I hope you're not suggesting I'd do anything to hurt Riley—"

"You brought that guy with the soul patch home after you'd only known him for thirty minutes. Riley woke up early, went to the kitchen for some chocolate milk, and stumbled upon him making himself coffee. He was wearing your nightie and nothing else!"

"I already apologised for that. Logan is a really

sweet guy, and an elementary school teacher. She wasn't in any danger."

"How would you know?"

"Because I know people and I'm never wrong."

"Ha," she says dismissively.

I feel anger bubbling up inside me. Kyle/Karl/Ken had at least two overnight stays before she'd known him a week, so I don't know how she dares comment on my relationships. I consider giving her a few home truths, but given how drunk and furious I am, there's a real possibility I'd be looking for a new home tomorrow if I did. Instead I turn to Richie. "If you needed me to pay more rent, you could have asked any time. We've been friends for two years." Richie swallows hard, his Adam's apple bulging against the neck of his t-shirt. I examine his body language: he looks tense, awkward and unhappy. He's still unable to make eye contact with me.

"Truth be told, I'm struggling a bit financially. The theatre hasn't made much money this month. Ticket sales were down on last quarter, and after we were robbed back in February . . . well, a little more rent would be helpful."

"Tell me how much you need, and I'll arrange it." There's sharpness in my tone, but as it perfectly reflects how pissed I am, I don't try to soften it.

"Thank you," he says. "But only if you can manage. You do have the smallest room – even smaller than Riley's."

Peyton rolls her eyes at him, then stands up to leave. An army of angry words rushes from my throat to my tongue. I bite my lip to stop them escaping. Have I been a shitty roommate as well as

16

a shitty friend? I remember all the times I've babysat Riley, as well as the nights I've stayed up talking into the small hours while she cried over one of her exes. Hell, I even passed up the chance of an audition because I knew she wanted the part. I *thought* I'd been a good friend to her, but maybe I haven't.

"I'm sorry if I've been inconsiderate, Peyton," I say. She stops walking and turns around to face me. "I certainly didn't intend to take advantage, but you could have spoken to me about it with kindness."

Her eyes water and her body shakes a little, but her resolve doesn't wane. "You're always so full of yourself that the only way to get through to you is by being direct."

I let yet more of her insults wash over me. "Peyton, I'm going to let you go to bed before I say something I might regret."

She takes hold of the door handle, poised to make her bid for freedom. "There's never a right time with you. We never know where you're going to be from one minute to the next: college, the diner, the theatre, clubs and bars, date after date after date. If your American dream has died it's through exhaustion from trying to keep up with you." She opens the door and starts to walk through it, but then she turns back. "You have more talent than any of us, so you only have yourself to blame if you don't have the life you want."

She slams the door shut and my heart simultaneously leaps into my throat. I've never felt as strong a connection with Peyton as I have with JJ or Richie, but I still considered her a close friend. I've always been there for her, and I thought she was there for me.

"Hey, you okay?" JJ moves his hand to my back and gives it a gentle pat.

"Not really," I reply. My vision is blurry and I try not to blink. The last thing I want to do is cry.

"I'm sorry, Freja." Richie moves to the armchair Peyton was sitting in opposite me. "I told Peyton about my finances. All the rest of the stuff she said was her grievances, not mine."

"But you didn't stand up for me."

"It's not as easy as that."

"Why not? Because she's your ex?"

"Yes, and because I don't want to upset either of you."

"Never mind, Richie. You don't need to explain."

"Forget about it," JJ says. He tucks his head into the crook of my neck and gives me a hug. "She's just jealous because she isn't as talented as you."

The last thing Peyton said to me tonight was I had more talent than the rest of them. Is he right? Is that what this whole thing is about – jealousy?

"Come on." JJ gives me another hug and tops up my glass with what's left of the pina colada. "How about we get this party started back up?"

I chew over Peyton's words. I left Denmark intent on having the time of my life. My career may not have taken off, but the best part of my life is embodied by the friends I've made. I'm twenty-five years old; I shouldn't be worrying about my future, I should be living my life with parties, no-strings sex and as much alcohol as my stomach can hold.

I leap to my feet. "Okay, I've had it with you three miserable jerks. We need to celebrate being alive. No more worrying about money or careers or relationships. These are supposed to be the best days of our lives! We're young, we have each other and we're all blessed with fabulousness!"

A smile erupts on JJ's face, making the hairs on his scratchy orange beard stand to attention. "Damn straight, we're fabulous. What the hell are we waiting for?"

"I'll crank up the music," says Aaron.

"And I'll refill the pitcher," says Richie. "I bought strawberries today. Let me shake us up some daiquiris."

"Now you're talking. If I'm going to have a hangover tomorrow, best make it a good one." I stand up and wobble a bit, but my head actually seems a bit clearer. "I'm sure I'll be able to manage at least three strawberry daiquiris before I fall into a coma. Leave the entertainment to me. I'm going to put a smile on all your faces tonight if it's the last thing I do."

I go to my room and hunt for the sexy elf outfit that delighted a room full of gay guys at JJ and Aaron's Christmas party. The top part of the costume disintegrated in the dryer, but I still have the shorts . . . somewhere. After fifteen minutes of searching I finally find them stuffed in a shoebox on the second shelf of my closet. They're made from red velvet, which is a little festive, but they're a perfect match for my . . . well, "top" would be misleading – they're a perfect match for the two teeny-tiny stickers Riley gave me to say sorry for scribbling on my Fendi handbag with black crayon.

I stick Mickey Mouse on my left boob and Minnie Mouse on the right.

Then I take a deep breath and tiptoe out of my bedroom, planning the details of my surprise with every step. The music coming from the living room is so loud I half expect our neighbours to call the cops, and . . . oh, isn't that typical? They've left the door open. Never mind. I can improvise.

I swing behind the door just as the music switches to "Crazy" by Gnarls Barkley. Perfect. How did the iPod know? I reattach Minnie's nose to my nipple and make my grand entrance.

"Ta-da!" I bound – or rather, I bounce – into the room.

And I come face to face with the most drop-dead gorgeous guy I have ever seen in my entire life.

I forget I'm standing there half naked as I give him the once-over – warm tanned skin, incredible dark eyes, and sandy-brown hair that is brushed away from his face in soft, choppy waves. The guy stares unapologetically at my tits and a delicious cheeky grin spreads across his face. "Am I in Disneyland?"

For fuck's sake. "I'm sorry. I was trying to perk—I mean cheer . . . Crap."

"Don't be sorry," says the hot guy, who possesses a hot English accent and a smile that looks like it's been made from vanilla-bean honey blended with sex endorphins. "I've just got off an eleven-hour flight and there's no better welcome to America than this. Have you got Donald Duck stuck anywhere?"

The guy's eyes skirt around my barely-there elf shorts.

"Are you done gawking?" I shout over the music.

A slightly embarrassed Richie steps forward. "Um, Freja, meet Nate."

Great. It would be, wouldn't it? Richie talks about Nate Klein as if he were a platinum-selling rock star. They met at Oxford, and Nate owns the lion's share of Richie's theatre. Why did I have to be half naked to finally meet him? *Well done, Freja. Well freaking done.*

"Nate is here to see Aaron. His company, Klein & Co, is huge in the tech world." As if I need the mini bio. "Freja rents our third bedroom."

Nate's eyes finally head north and lock onto mine. "Hi, Freja," he says, beaming me a huge smile. He offers me his hand, and despite never feeling embarrassed about being naked at any point in my life previously, I suddenly want the ground to swallow me up. I cover my tits with one of my arms and shake his hand.

"I should go and get dressed." My cheeks warm up. For fuck's sake, why am I blushing? Half the students at UCLA and most people with a Myspace account have seen my tits.

Nate laughs from his belly. "I'm sorry, but this is hilarious."

"What, are you fifteen?" I put my hands on my hips and inhale a confident breath. "Okay, you've seen my body, so deal with it."

As I spin around, I realise my elf shorts barely cover my ass, but I waltz out of the room with my head held high regardless.

2

THE LAST THING I REMEMBER is putting on a pair of PJs and crashing onto my bed. I fully intended to go back downstairs, but five minutes' rest somehow turned into all freaking night. The bright Californian sunshine streams in through my bedroom window, attacking my hungover eyes, and I pull a pillow over my head. I wish I could stay in bed all day, but I have a shift at the Cosmic Diner at twelve. I do some maths. Yes! I don't need to get up until eleven fifteen. I can totally shower and dress in ten minutes. I've done it before, several times, and always with a hangover.

I turn over, moving my legs into the cool, unslept-in area of my bed. I stretch out until my joints groan with ecstasy. Then I reset my alarm. Thank goodness the house is quiet. Aaron and JJ will have headed home at some point during the night, and Riley must still be at her grandparents'. The most important consideration, of course, is whether Nate is still here.

My stomach flips when I think about how good-looking he was, but I order my brain not to go there. I'm probably still drunk, and he probably isn't as incredibly hot, charming and breathtakingly alluring as I remember. Blurry memories of his dark eyes, tall physique, crisp accent and sexy grin float into my mind, refusing to budge until I've indulged myself by thinking about him some more. I've been intrigued by the legendary Nate Klein for ages and, judging by what my body is doing when I think about him, he's left an impression I wasn't expecting.

Nate and Richie moved to California and bought the Sunshine Theatre six years ago, but Nate returned to England eighteen months before I answered Richie and Peyton's ad for a roommate. I've seen photos of him, but he's even better-looking in the flesh. And oh my god, I wish I could stop thinking about him, because I need to go back to sleep. I scrunch my eyes shut and concentrate on seeing black, but up pops Nate's face again. Or rather, up pop his deep dark eyes . . . and his delicious smile . . . and fuck it, who am I kidding? I'm going to have to go where my brain is taking me . . . and it seems as though it's taking me to a wonderful place where Nate's bronzed body is naked and covered in oil.

Jesus! Hvad er der galt med mig? What's wrong with me?

I push my thighs together to stifle the intense ache in my groin. I live in Santa Monica; I'm surrounded by hot men every single day of my life. There are surfers, swimmers, between-job actors – even the cops and workmen are hot. So what's so special about this guy? The pulsating throb between my legs deepens until I give in to the longing and slide a hand under my pyjama bottoms and get to work. I caress my breast with the other hand and . . . holy shit, I definitely won't be needing any assistance from my Rampant Rabbit this morning. On the one hand, this is good news because I think my batteries are flat. But on the other hand, this is

23

very, very bad news. The worst news. I can't remember the last time I felt this horny over a virtual stranger. In fact, I don't think I've *ever* felt this horny in my life.

* * *

"Freja, Freja, wake up!"

I shoot bolt upright in my bed. Crap, how long was I asleep? I push my hair out of my face and focus on the digits on my alarm clock. There's a ten. Thank goodness for that. And there are zeroes after the ten. Even better – I have an hour.

"Freja, look what Grandma got me," says the chirpy voice outside my door. "You're gonna love it!"

"Just a minute, sweetie."

I adjust my PJs and rub at my cheeks. I'm not sure my skin is attached to my face. I get out of bed and gawp at my reflection in the wall mirror. Ugh. I look like I've been sleeping in a cornfield, and my hair looks as though it belongs to the hobo who lives in Palisades Park. And I *still* feel tired. I've had an extra two hours of sleep and I've given myself an orgasm that would have inspired Madonna to rewrite "Like a Virgin". I should be feeling far more energised than this.

"Freja! I am getting really tired of waiting!" Riley's little voice has reached level ten on the "squawky and demanding" scale. I forget about fixing my hair and open the door to find my smallest friend grinning from ear to ear. She's holding something behind her back. "Close your

24

eyes." I hunker down on my knees. "Okay, now you can look," she says with a delightful squeal and a flurry of giggles.

"You got another Ariel?"

She nods. "This one comes with a pink party dress!"

The three-year-old thrusts the Disney Princess doll into my hand. "Wow, she's super cute, Riley."

"Because she's you!"

I once told Riley that the Little Mermaid is a Danish girl, just like me, and showed her a picture of the statue in Copenhagen. I didn't expect her to take my comment literally, but, probably due to my red hair, she's now totally convinced I'm a real-life mermaid. I always play along because you're only three once, right?

"She has a fabulous bikini top," I say approvingly. "I need one of those."

Riley frowns. "You *should* already have one."

Åh Gud. Come on, Freja. Keep the dream alive. Think. "Yes, but I can only wear it when I have my mermaid tail and I'm swimming in the sea." I give her a reassuring hug which thankfully makes her smile return. "I need another one for sunbathing in the back yard."

"Ahhhh." Her eyes light up with excitement. I should add the invention of top-secret mermaid information to my résumé. Riley's a lucky girl. When I was three, our cat killed a mouse, so my dad took the opportunity to introduce me to the wonders of rodent anatomy. Hans Larsen is one of a kind. He taught me to stand out from the crowd, and that's a lesson which has always served me well in life.

I hand Riley her doll back. "So, what adventures

do you have planned today?"

"I have dance class. Mommy sent me upstairs to get my tap shoes." She stops talking and checks out her doll's feet. "It must be hard for mermaids to dance."

"Erm . . . yeah, it is."

"You're a great dancer, Freja. I'm glad you have feet now, because if you still had a tail, you wouldn't be able to go downstairs and dance with Prince Eric."

"Do you mean Uncle Richie?"

"No, I mean Prince Eric. Uncle Richie's best friend."

Oh crap, does she mean Nate? Did he stay the night? If I see him before breakfast does that mean I'll spend the rest of the day imagining his gorgeous body wrapped up in my tangled bed sheets?

"Riley, have you got your shoes on?" Peyton calls from downstairs. She sounds as angry as she did last night. "Come on, kiddo. We have to leave the house in two minutes!"

Riley's blue eyes fill with anxious tears. "Mommy's getting mad. Will you help me find my tap shoes?"

I follow her into her bedroom and head straight for the closet. Riley's room is fluffy, sparkly and filled from floor to ceiling with pink plastic toys. Her carbon footprint must be off the scale and she hasn't even started school yet. I open her closet doors and a menagerie of cupcake-coloured stuffed animals fly out at me. No wonder she can't find anything. "Where did you last see your shoes?"

"On my feet."

"Yeah, thanks Riley, very helpful." I start pulling

26

out toys, clothes and, ugh, empty juice boxes from her closet. The kid is a slob. I pile the junk back onto her shelves, then I spot something silver, glittery and shoe-like under her bed.

"You know, you could try keeping your room clean." She stares at me as if I'm speaking in Japanese.

I shuffle under the bed on my belly and, because the world hates me, my cheap polyester pyjama top decides to have a weird reaction to the nylon carpet. Ouch. We could power the house with static electricity . . . and great, just freaking great. My top rolls up to my neck and there's no space for me to angle my arms to pull it back down. Fuck it, I'll just have to go with it. I reach for the nearest shoe and throw it out from under the bed.

"Yay! You found them," says Riley.

"Correction, I found one." I don't tell her I've given my tits carpet burns in the process. Why is her bed so damned low? Crap, now I can't move. I'm wedged in by all the plastic Barbie garbage and shoeboxes full of McDonald's Happy Meal toys and . . . what the . . . ? So that's where my glitter nail polish disappeared to. "I can see your other shoe, Riley . . . Ouch, fu—" I stop myself just in time.

"Did you say a bad word?"

"No, I got poked in the eye by Barbie's horse's foot." Damn, that thing's got a spikey hoof.

"It sounded like a bad word."

"Well, it wasn't."

Why didn't I send Riley under the bed? She's three, which means she's smaller than I am. I twist to the left and my nipple grazes something sharp. I shriek in agony.

"Freja, are you okay? Did you hurt your eye again?"

"No, I'm stuck." I pull a metal pencil sharpener from under my boob. "You're cleaning your room when you get back from your dance class, young lady."

With the last remaining shoe in sight, I wriggle further into the abyss and give it everything I've got, which may or may not include a pulled muscle judging by the snapping noise in my shoulder.

"Do you need any help?"

A voice I absolutely did not want to hear booms into the room.

Åh, lort. Nej, nej, nej! Why is he still here? Why is he upstairs? And why does the world hate me? I ignore the pain in my shoulder and toss the shoe towards him. "No, thank you. I'm done."

"I think Freja has hurt herself. Are you Prince Eric? Are you going to kiss her now? Will you have a mermaid baby so I can play with her? She could live in the bath tub!"

Jesus Christ, has she been possessed by the devil? She didn't even stop for air when she delivered that vomit of humiliation into the room.

"Riley, are you ready to go?" Peyton yells again. "Uncle Richie is waiting to give us a ride in his car. We're too late to walk now."

"Coming, Mommy," she says. I hear her trot out of the room, then her footsteps pit-pat down the stairs. Finally, the door slams shut.

Silence. Is Nate still here?

"Are you sure you don't need any help?"

Damn it.

"No, it's okay. I've had a wardrobe malfunction."

"Well, here, let me help y—"

"I said I was fine!" *Min Gud! Is he intentionally trying to make me cringe to my toes?*

I see a pair of black-and-pink checked Vans move around Riley's bed. "Are you . . . ? Do you have your clothes off again?"

"No, my clothes are on!" My tone is probably a bit too snippy given I am technically naked from the waist up. "I told you already. I've had a wardrobe malfunction." I try to twist my butt around ninety degrees, but I only have a millimetre of wiggle room and . . . argh! What the hell? My hair is caught on something.

"Okay, this is silly. Let me move some of this stuff."

I fumble around my head. Somehow my hair has become knotted around a metal screw in the bed frame. This has to be the most humiliating experience of my life. Nate begins to pull Riley's junk out from under the bed, and I want to die. Ten seconds later, he's lying on the floor opposite me, staring directly into my lust-stricken soul.

"Your hair is all caught up," he says, stating the blatantly obvious. He rolls onto his side and shuffles towards me.

"What are you doing?" I yelp in agony as my head jerks away from him.

"Untangling you," he says with a shrug. His legs slide under the bed and rest against mine. The ever-so-slight clothed contact between his chinos and my pyjama pants makes my vagina pulsate with pleasure.

29

"*Det her er mit livs værste dag*!" This is definitely the worst day of my life.

"Erm, what?"

"Sorry, just talking to myself." I sigh in defeat and let him continue. "I think I broke my arm."

His body smiles. And when I say his body smiles, I mean his *body* smiles. His eyes, his brows, his thick eyelashes, his warm olive skin, even his hair . . . He might just be the only person on the planet who can smile with non-face-related body parts.

"If you'd broken your arm you'd know about it," he says, yanking me out of my swoon.

"Well, it hurts."

"Don't move. I can only do one thing at a time. Let's get your hair free first."

He slides in closer and begins carefully separating my hair from the metal screws. He's so close his breath tickles the exposed skin of my shoulder. My reproductive organs hook up with each other and dance a slow dance. I yawn into the carpet. "I hadn't brushed my hair yet." He untwists a matted lock of hair and it falls in front of my face. Shit, it looks like it's been coughed up by a cat. After it's killed a mouse. "I've just woken up. It was a . . . um . . . busy night, last night."

"You can say that again." He gives me a cheeky wink, and my pathetically weak stomach flips over again.

"Whatever do you mean?" I say, knowing exactly what he means.

"Put it this way: I didn't expect to be greeted by an X-rated version of *The Mickey Mouse Club* when I dropped by last night." He gives my hair one final tug, then he gently smoothes it over my shoulder, letting his fingers linger just a little bit too long. His gaze sparkles. "So, um, do you want me to help with your broken arm now?"

"Can you do it with your eyes closed?"

He smirks. "There's nothing under there that I didn't see last night. Do you want me to try to adjust your top?"

"No, just pull me out." He takes hold of my arm. "What are you doing? Are you crazy? Don't pull my broken arm! Pull my legs."

His head dips to one side. "Sorry." He gets up off the floor and disappears out of my line of vision. I take a deep breath and prepare myself for more carpet burns. I hear him move Riley's doll stroller and wooden dollhouse, then he takes hold of my legs and pulls and . . . oh, sweet Jesus, the burn. I need something frozen and I need it now, and I need to wear it on my chest for a week.

I push my pyjama top down and sit up. "Thank you." He leans against the doorframe, his entire body doing that smiling thing again. I notice the hard outline of his torso under his white t-shirt and my vagina starts beating in sync with my heart. I really wish it would stop doing that. "Why are you looking at me like that?"

His smile grows wider. "Just wondering when you're going to admit that you're into me?"

What the hell? The cocky son of a . . . "I was trapped under a kid's bed, not a burning building. If you think that level of heroism is going to make me fall at your feet, then I think you're living in the wrong century."

"Whatever you say, Freja." I hear the front door

31

close, followed by Richie's footsteps. "I'll catch you later."

I stare at his ass as he walks away. What the hell am I getting myself into?

* * *

I shower, brush my hair and change into my work clothes. The Cosmic Diner is a retro eatery on the very historic Route 66. This means it's a mecca for tourists, and I'm required to dress in a skimpy waitress dress and wear roller skates for the best part of my shift. The tips are great, so I don't completely hate my job, but having to wear an outfit that has appeared in every male customer's wet dreams takes its toll.

I scrape up my hair into a long, loose ponytail and tie my stiff white apron around my waist. Then I go to the kitchen and grab a banana and a bowl of muesli. When I walk into the living room, Nate and Richie are deep in conversation. They stop talking when they see me.

"Nate was just telling me you got stuck under Riley's bed." Richie laughs and runs his fingers along his trim beard. I glance at Nate. He's smiling, but it's different than before. His eyes are empty and there's something strange and hard and unhappy hanging in the air.

"What's going on, guys?" I plonk my cereal bowl down on the coffee table.

"Nothing," says Richie. He gives me a fake smile, then his face changes and he sighs deeply. "I've never been able to keep anything from you,

32

have I?"

Richie's admission makes Nate sit up straight. "What do you mean?"

I start to peel my banana. "He means I can read him. I can read you too."

"Oh, really?" He reclines on the sofa, crossing one leg over the other. Damn him, he even crosses his legs smugly. "What am I thinking, then?"

I narrow my eyes and scan him from head to toe. I deliberately let my eyes linger on his lips, then his chest, as he watches me closely. I wait and eventually he delivers. Nobody else would have noticed the ever-so-slight self-conscious shift in his body language: he pulls at his sleeve, swallows hard and finally breaks eye contact. Got him.

"You slept on our sofa, instead of in your five-star hotel room, for a reason. You're feeling guilty about something." I take a bite of my banana while Nate constructs what he probably thinks is the perfect poker face – it isn't. "You're here on business and you weren't planning to be in the States for long, but there's something personal you want to take care of first. You're sitting close to Richie because he's your top priority." I harden my stare and his eyes begin to betray him. "You're tough, but you're a pleaser. You care about what people think of you. You don't want people to think you're a bad guy."

Nate's dark eyes are fixed on mine. I don't avert my gaze and neither does he.

"I told you she was something else," says Richie.

Nate doesn't speak. His olive skin darkens, but his expression is conflicted. One of his cheeks dimples as a barely noticeable smile dances across his lips, but his eyes tell a story of sadness and remorse.

I turn to Richie. "So, are you going to tell me what's going on?"

Richie glances briefly at his friend before answering. "Nate's father has just made him managing director of the family business, but on the proviso that he proves his long-term commitment. He has to sell his interest in the theatre."

Richie's words ignite a fire in my belly. "That's bullshit."

Nate bristles. "Look, Freja, clearly you think you know me, but you don't." He raises his voice. "You also don't know my father. Investing in the theatre was always a loan. Richie knew this day would come."

"So you're just going to destroy his livelihood?"

"Freja," Richie says sharply.

I hold up my hands in despair. "This is incredible. How long are you going to give him to find another investor?"

"Four weeks."

I laugh. "Four weeks, and then what?"

"I have interest from a development company who want to turn it into a casino."

Jesus, I want to kill him so badly.

"The theatre is failing," says Richie. "We're losing money every month, and my acting career isn't doing all that great either. Maybe it's time to cut my losses."

"You *love* the theatre, and you know Hollywood is hard. We all do. The theatre has been the only thing that's kept you going."

"It's fine, Freja," says Richie, his eyes downcast.

34

"Whatever happens, happens. I'll be okay. Nate has given me five years, and I've given Sunshine my best shot, but like you said, this business . . ." His voice gets lost and he swallows hard. "It's tough."

I glare at Nate. "Give him eight weeks."

"I can't," says Nate. "I don't know if the development company will hang around—"

"They'll hang around if they want it badly enough. You're supposed to be a high-flying hotshot businessman, aren't you? If you're as great as your father thinks you are, you should be able to negotiate another month. Richie deserves it."

Nate's demeanour softens. "Yeah, I know he deserves it."

"Good. Now I have to get to work." I stand up and straighten my uniform. The apron has a gigantic crease down the middle. I attempt to iron it out with my palms.

"Have dinner with me next week?"

"What?" I say with a gasp. Is he for real?

"Have dinner with me next week and Richie gets his two months."

Richie laughs. "That might not be the best way to ask a girl out, mate."

Nate's face blanches. "Oh god, I'm sorry." His eyes widen and he shakes his head. "The eight weeks thing is unrelated to dinner, of course. You've got the time already."

I raise an eyebrow and start to walk away.

"Is that a yes?" he calls after me.

"I'll think about it."

3

WHEN I MOVED TO CALIFORNIA two years ago, I enrolled on a part-time film and television master's course at UCLA. I was committed to making it as an actress, but student visas are much easier to obtain than work visas, so the logistics of my new life led me here.

In two weeks' time my second year as a part-time graduate student comes to an end. This officially gives me just one more year to study, and I have no idea what comes next. JJ complains endlessly about my lack of direction. He plans everything down to the last detail, probably because he's a part-time litigator as well as a part-time student, while my life amounts to a mishmash of unpredictable and spontaneous events interlinked by chaos. I don't know where I'm going until I get there, but the journey is where I find the excitement, not the destination. You find out who you are when you throw yourself into a gigantic mess and make something wonderful out of it.

"You're late again!" JJ yells at me across half a row of lecture hall seats. His arms are folded crossly around his body.

"Watch out, guys, coming through." Most of my classmates either stand up or move their legs to let me past, but one of them appears to have a death wish. "You touch my ass one more time, Rico Kaminski, and I *will* hurt you."

"Hey, if you don't want the customers to touch, you need to put a sign on the goods."

"I should put a sign on my ass? How the hell would that work?" I say to the musicology major whose teeth look like they've taken a bath in green tea mixed with nicotine extract. "Fortunately, you'd have to pay someone to touch your goods."

The hall erupts into cheers, and Rico's skin reddens over a fake smile. The guy's a total moron, so I'm not remotely sorry.

Today's lecture is being given by self-professed "man of the people" Reed McHale, a film director with Twilight Studios. Over the years, we've been treated to guest lectures from a variety of Hollywood people, including award-winning producers and big-name actors, but Reed's lectures always seem to draw the biggest crowd. Sadly, this has more to do with his off-colour jokes and hatred of political correctness than the actual educational content of his lectures.

Reed walks to the podium, front and centre of the lecture hall. He's a tall Texan with weathered skin, a stubbly beard and jeans that are too loose for his body. His Motorhead t-shirt and biker jacket contribute to the "edgy and cool" vibe he's keen to project. He flicks a button on the podium, and the huge screen behind him sparkles to life: "How political correctness is poisoning America's movie industry." As soon as the words fill the hall, half the room jeers and whistles their approval while the other half, including me and JJ, groan and eye-roll ourselves into oblivion.

Count me out. I pull my baseball cap down and fire up my cell phone. "Wake me up when it's over," I whisper to JJ.

"Sure thing, sis."

I switch my phone's sound off and click on my notifications. Great, just what I need. Another text message and probably another dinner invitation from Nate Klein. It's been two days since he asked me out, and although my vagina desperately wants to experience a hot date with this hot man, my brain is telling me to keep my distance. And I'm choosing to avoid him for five very good reasons. Reason one: Nate's in the middle of a hugely important business deal with Aaron. Two: he's my roommate's best friend. Three: he's only going to be in the US short term. Four: his father sounds like a cross between Gordon Gekko and Dolores Umbridge. And five: I'm terrified of how he makes me feel.

And it feels weak and not like me to acknowledge something like that, but it's true. He makes me feel like I could lose myself, and as much as I enjoy chaos and mess and spontaneity in my life, when it comes to relationships I want to feel in control.

I know what losing control in love looks like. It looks like abandoning your children to go and live in Monaco with a property developer. It looks like *her*, and I will never be like her. And that's why I married Per Christiansen when I was nineteen. Per was stable and secure – a solid bridge between my splintered childhood and the kind of future I thought I wanted. He was a cosy cup of hot chocolate as opposed to an exciting glass of champagne, but I convinced myself that warm fireside chats and long walks in the forest with a loyal partner were what I needed.

I go to my messages and remind myself that if Nate Klein were a beverage, he'd be a ten-grand bottle of vintage Dom Pérignon. I do not want that in my life, but my god, my body is protesting.

NATE: I was wondering if you'd given any more thought to dinner? Are you free tonight?

JJ peeps over my shoulder as Reed McHale's dull voice drones on in the background like Charlie Brown's schoolteacher. I sink down in my seat and show him my phone.

"Are you going to say yes?" JJ whispers.

"I don't know. What do you think?"

"I think he's hot, and we've always had the same taste in men, so that means you must think he's hot too."

"You do realise you have a boyfriend who's in a meeting with Nate right now, don't you?"

JJ shrugs. "So? Aaron thinks he's hot too."

A Latino girl with a mass of corkscrew curls turns around and shushes us. JJ scrunches up his nose and pokes out his tongue, because he's *that* mature.

I reply to Nate's message: *I was planning on washing my hair*. Then I cringe. Are the old lines still the best?

NATE: Do you need any help? I'm already very well acquainted with your hair. And a couple of your other things.

I gasp. I show JJ my phone, and his mouth falls open. "He's talking about Mickey and Minnie, isn't he? Damn, sis, he's a cocky bastard, but he's scorching."

"Bro, you have a point. I might be in trouble."

As much as I'm outraged, my need to get the better of Nate compels me to up the ante in the flirting stakes: *I hope you enjoyed your view, because you won't be seeing them again.*

"You sure about that?" says JJ, peering over my shoulder with eyebrows raised. "Half of Los Angeles has seen your tits."

"I'm trying to be demure. Are you suggesting I invite him over to play with them?"

He holds his hands up. "It would save time in the long run."

I shake my head. With friends like JJ, who needs enemies?

Another message comes through. I angle my phone away from JJ's prying eyes.

NATE: I'm only here a few more weeks and I really want to eat you. What do you say?

I squint at my phone. He wants to eat me? Did he *really* just say he wants to eat me? What hellish abyss of perviness am I smut-texting my way into here?

"What's up?" asks JJ.

"Nothing," I say quickly. The disgust must be plastered all over my face.

I try to catch up with the lecture. Reed McHale is delivering a sermon disputing that Hollywood is guilty of whitewashing black characters. I tune out again and return to my phone, but I have no idea how to reply. Has he made a typo or is he just a jerk?

Thankfully, a new message swiftly arrives shedding light on the last one: *Oh my fucking god, what did my phone just say?*

A second later I receive another: *I am so sorry. I*

swear I wrote "I really want to date you," not "eat" you. Most embarrassing autocorrect ever.

My body explodes into giggles. I sink further down in my chair and adjust my cap so it obscures my face from the world.

ME: Ah, you're going with the old autocorrect excuse?

NATE: Yes. I always tell the truth.

Hmm, does he? Maybe he's hot chocolate after all.

ME: Okay then. I'll accept your dinner offer. Where are you taking me?

Two minutes of silence pass before I receive the next message: *For real?*

ME: Yes. I always tell the truth too.

What was I saying earlier about trust and loyalty? My stomach starts to spin. Is my brain finally on the same side as my vagina?

NATE: I'll pick you up at eight. I should have recovered from my run by then. Genital Park is brutal. My handjobs are killing me.

Holy shit! Please, God, if you're listening, never ever let this man get better at texting. I laugh again, but this time I don't hide it as well and I'm caught.

"Is something amusing you, Miss Larsen?" Reed McHale bellows across the lecture room.

My phone vibrates once, twice, three times. Crap.

"No, Mr McHale. I'm listening intently." I don't feel guilty about lying. Reed's silly lecture is little more than a rant from a privileged white guy mourning a time when it was acceptable to be a bigoted prick.

"Come see me after the lecture."

41

I nod my head. Great. Just freaking great. Do grad students get detention? Another three vibrations wake up my cell.

NATE: Jesus Christ, I want to die! I did not write those words.

NATE: Griffith Park not Genital Park. GRIFFITH.

NATE: Shit and hell. My hamstrings are killing me, not handjobs.

NATE: Excuse me while I kill my phone.

NATE: Do you still want to eat me?

NATE: FUCK!!! Date me! DATE, DATE, DATE!!!

I chew on the neck of my t-shirt. This must be the worst yet best text conversation in the history of the world.

ME: I agreed to dinner, but I don't want you to eat me and I'm not massaging your handjobs. Genital Park sounds fun though. If there're swings and ice cream, I'm in.

I laugh inwardly at my own jokes. Could I be any funnier? Sign me up for *Saturday Night Live* already.

He replies with a smiley face, which I read as confirmation of my fabulousness.

* * *

When the lecture ends, I wait behind as Reed McHale asked. As I watch everyone leave the hall, I try to think of a good excuse, but I can't, so I figure I'll just come clean and make a half-assed apology.

When we're alone, I do a quick scan of Reed.

He's standing uneasily and his brow is creased. He certainly looks very anxious. Weird. I wasn't expecting this.

"Mr McHale, before you say anything, I have no excuse for mucking about during your lecture. It was very rude of me and I promise it won't happen again." I smile as sweetly as I can.

Reed waves away my apology. "That isn't why I wanted to see you," he says in his distinctive Texas drawl.

"Oh?" I ask, intrigued by the wave of nervousness in his voice. I'm so used to McHale being an arrogant loudmouth.

He leans against the lecture podium, one arm resting near the mic. "I'm part way through shooting a movie with Twilight Studios, but one of my actresses has just walked off set. I need to replace her and I have no time for auditions. I wondered if you'd be interested."

My heart skips a beat. "Are you serious?" I say, my voice is so high with excitement that I'm practically squealing.

Reed's smile widens, but he still has tension in his eyes. "You have movie experience, and you impressed me when you played Cordelia in last year's end-of-year-show. I'm not a Shakespeare fan, but you really nailed it."

"Thank you. I loved doing that play."

"I could tell." He opens up his leather messenger bag and takes out a stack of papers. "The character – Maya – is a redhead and she's Eastern European, so I thought of you straight away."

"I'm from Denmark."

He looks at me blankly. "That's in Europe,

43

right?"

"Yes, but north, not east."

"Near enough," he says, grinning broadly. "We need someone with an accent, and it's a great opportunity. If you agree, I need you on set from Friday, which means you'll miss the last week of college, but I'll square it with the dean." He thumbs through the papers and passes me a script entitled *Twisted Street*. "It's a straight-to-TV movie, but it's already been bought by a premium cable channel."

My excitement wanes a little. I was imagining a cinematic release. I flick through the script, and a few choice words don't so much leap out at me as grab hold of my stomach and tie it in a knot. "Um, what kind of film is this?"

"Ah, the dreaded question." Reed stands tall and puffs out his chest. "Look, I'll level with you here, and you can say no if it's not your thing, but *Twisted Street* is an erotic suspense thriller adapted from a bestselling novel. When I said I knew you had movie experience, I meant that I knew you had *this* kind of movie experience."

In Copenhagen, I was cast in a Scandi noir TV series playing a young police officer with a fetish for screwing male prisoners. One of them ended up strangling her to death. "You mean you checked my résumé to see if I'd do nudity?"

"Yeah, sorry." He tilts his head and smiles. "Truth be told, you were already on my radar after King Lear. Like I said before, you really impressed me."

"I have an agent. I should probably run this past her."

"By all means, but I need an answer by

tomorrow. I'm using my own cash to help fund the movie and I can't afford delays in shooting. My last three films have tanked, so my ass is on the line with this one. I have four days to fill the role."

Crap. Should I go for it? I'm not bothered in the slightest about the nudity and I know my career needs this, but I don't want a borderline soft-porn movie coming back to haunt me if I ever do make it big in Hollywood. "Okay, give me the lowdown. How many sex scenes?"

"Five. Two in a bed, one in a shower, one featuring a kitchen counter and one in the backseat of a Camaro."

Oh shit. At least he's being honest. "Fully nude?"

He nods. "Three out of the five. We'll shoot on a closed set. Just you, me, the male actor and a reduced crew of professional union members."

"And the other scenes?"

"Your character gets stabbed to death in the bathtub, and then there's a scene in the mortuary. Most of you would be covered by a sheet in that one, though."

I laugh. "Great. That will make *all* the difference."

Reed laughs too. "Yeah, I know this is a bit weird. If it helps we've cast a couple of big names in the lead roles. Julia Bowman is coming from network soap operas, and Todd Warner has guested in several prime-times. The movie has great buzz already due to the book's popularity."

I haven't heard of the book, but it sounds like the sort of badly written sensationalist crap Peyton devours. Can I do this? I'm sure I can. I feel like I should, if only to help out Richie financially. "How much?"

"Huh? Oh, you mean wage? Your predecessor negotiated five grand via her agent, which we'd honour."

Holy shit, that's more than I expected. "Make it ten and I'll do it."

"Wow, you're going to come right out and ask for double, just like that?" He sounds shocked, but he looks impressed. "You're an unknown, and it's a relatively minor part."

"You're asking me to go nude as well as simulate sex, so I think ten grand is more than fair."

"I can go to six."

"I want ten."

"I could get someone cheaper."

"She wouldn't be me. Ten and you have your actress."

Reed runs his fingers over his short beard and bites his lip. "Damn, you're good. Eight."

I extend my hand. "Deal."

"I look forward to working with you, Miss Larsen," says Reed. He shakes my hand firmly and gives me a business card. "I'll have a contract sent over this afternoon. Call my assistant if there's anything you need."

"I will, thank you. It was fun negotiating with you."

"You too."

I'm so ecstatic when I leave the hall that I'm halfway home before I remember Reed McHale is a repellent windbag who believes Hollywood has a wicked agenda to turn American men into "soft effeminate pussies". Oh well, it's best I don't think too much about that now.

* * *

I get home from college and settle down to read through my script. I looked up the book, and its buzz, on Google. Although the writing is cringey-bad, the story seems quite thrilling. My character, Maya, is a Russian kindergarten teacher and secret spy (yes, really) who is having an illicit affair with her hot but unbelievably dim next-door neighbour, Drew.

On paper, Maya is a walking, talking stereotype and as one-dimensional as a piece of cardboard. I persevere through the entire script to try to get a good sense of who she is, but I have to create my own backstory and identity for her because she's written solely to be used as a sex object. Sad to think that women are writing women in this way in the twenty-first century. Even sadder that female readers are enjoying it so much.

I'm just about to go upstairs to get ready for my date when Richie and Peyton arrive home with a very sleepy Riley. I can't wait to tell them my news. "Hi, guys," I say, moving my legs from the sofa to let them sit down. "I've got something I want to tell you both. Have you got a minute?"

"I need to give Riley her bath and get her into bed. She's been in daycare since seven," Peyton says.

Riley stretches out her arms and Peyton picks her up. "Too sleepy for bath, Mommy." She yawns into Peyton's hair.

"Okay, honey. You can go straight to bed tonight." Peyton carries Riley up the stairs, the little girl's arms wrapped tight around her neck.

Richie sits down next to me. His grim mood is palpable. "Things aren't looking too great with the theatre, Freja." He reaches out and takes my hand. His eyes are filled with sadness.

"I called my bank today. I can pay you an extra hundred dollars a month rent and—"

"That's not going to be enough. I've found a studio that says they might be able to sponsor us, but I still need to find three hundred thousand dollars to buy out Nate. I can only get a loan for twenty grand. My parents said they can give me another fifty, but I can't see any way . . . Maybe it's for the best."

"No." I give his hand a squeeze. "Let me talk to Nate."

Richie shakes his head. "You don't know him. He's a stand-up guy, but he's tough. Once he makes his mind up about something, he gets what he wants."

I feel like cancelling my date. "Even if that means stabbing his best friend in the back?"

Richie rakes a hand through his hair. His blue eyes are glassy and circled by dark shadows. "It was always meant to be a loan, Freja. I knew that five years ago, and I'm grateful Nate gave me a chance at doing something I love."

"I'm so sorry, Rich."

"I know, but these things happen. We still have some time, so maybe something will come up. There's a chance we could find another sponsor or investor, but it's a long shot."

Peyton enters the room and flops down in the adjacent armchair. "Riley fell asleep the second I put her in her pyjamas. God, what a day. My feet are killing me."

"Thanks for upping your shifts at the diner," says Richie. "You didn't have to. I'm really grateful."

"I know what the theatre means to you, Rich. We all need to up our game." Peyton's tone is laced thick with passive-aggression, which confirms she still has a problem with me. If she's still complaining that I'm not pulling my weight, my news should put an end to it.

I take a deep breath. "I have something to tell you guys." Their eyes fall on me. "I have a part in a TV movie."

Richie practically leaps off the sofa. "Wow, Freja, that's really great. I am so proud of you." He leans in and gives me a huge hug that almost knocks the air from my lungs. "What movie is it? How big is the part?"

I glance at Peyton. She looks like she's going to be sick. Since when was she this jealous? And why is she being so freaking obvious about it? "It's a key role. I have seven scenes in total. I'll be playing a sexy Russian spy."

"A spy? Woah, that's *so* you! You're going to kill it," says Richie.

"What's the movie?" asks Peyton.

My father always told me to watch the people who don't cheer when you're winning, and tonight Peyton is that person. I feel her resentment creep under my skin, and my blood curdles in my veins. "It's based on a book called *Twisted Street*. I'm playing a character called Maya and . . ." My words get lost in my throat when I notice the look on her face. "Have you read it?"

"*Twisted Street* is essentially soft porn, Freja," she says with a short, scoffing laugh. "All the daycare moms have read it. You did know this when you accepted the part, didn't you?"

My insides swirl with shame and insecurity. Why am I allowing her to make me feel like this? I summon up some strength. "Yes. I've read the script and I know what the role involves."

Richie looks between us, confusion embedded in his eyes. "What am I missing here?"

Peyton laughs. "You won't want to miss Freja's movie, that's for sure."

I open my mouth, ready to defend myself, but why the hell should I? "All three of us are actors. Sometimes roles call for nudity and sex scenes." I glance at Richie and notice the ridges of his frown deepen. "Are you saying neither of you would accept this kind of role?"

"I certainly wouldn't," says Peyton. She fixes me with the most self-righteous glare I've ever seen. "I don't mind showing the side of my breast or part of my ass, but let's get real here. *Twisted Street* is a low-rent porno novel. There's a graphic sex scene in every chapter, so it's obvious what kind of movie you'll be making."

"I negotiated a higher fee to reflect the sexual content." I even out my tone, but anger is still raging inside of me. She's doing everything she can to put down my choices. "I'm going to invest my entire paycheck – eight grand – in the theatre."

Richie shifts awkwardly next to me. "Freja, I love you and that's a really sweet gesture, but you don't have to do this."

"Eight grand is hardly worth selling yourself for," Peyton scoffs.

Richie's body stiffens. "Peyton, that's a step too far."

I take to my feet. "I don't know what crawled up your ass and died over these past few days, Peyton, but know this – there is nothing you can ever say that will make me doubt myself."

"The fact you're angry with me for questioning you means you're already doubting yourself," Peyton says with a fake smile.

"I don't have a problem with questions, but I do have a problem with insults." I walk towards the door. "Now, if you're done, I have a date tonight and I have to get ready."

"With who?"

"With Nate Klein. He's picking me up at eight."

Peyton's skin turns the colour of chalk. "So you're selling yourself to him too?"

"That's enough. Just stop now!" yells Richie.

"No, Peyton," I say, my tone thick with sarcasm. "I'm aiming to have the time of my life with a great-looking guy who's really into me. What will you be doing tonight?"

Hvorfor siger jeg det? Why am I saying this? I listen to the words coming out of my mouth and I hate myself for reacting. This isn't me. I don't let people get to me and I never defend my choices.

I stomp up the stairs and put Peyton out of my mind.

51

4

I PULL A BLACK TOP from my closet. When you're a natural redhead, life teaches you that many colours are not your friend, so over the years I've learned to trust black. And grey and white. Blues and greens come out for special occasions. Red and pink hate me, and as for orange? Don't even go there.

From behind my bedroom door I can hear Richie and Peyton arguing downstairs. In the two years we've lived together, I've never felt uncomfortable around them. Sure, there's been the odd squabble, but it's never been this bad. I considered Peyton my closest girlfriend as well as my roomie and co-worker. I sometimes forget she and Richie were once together romantically, because they're such great mates. Richie is kind-hearted and practical, with a wealth of classical theatre training behind him. Peyton is cool and self-assured, with a résumé headlined by a dozen commercials. They've been able to form a solid post-romantic relationship because they were once each other's cup of familiar and supportive hot chocolate.

I bend over and throw my hair forward so I can tie the straps of my halterneck top. The strapless bra is already pinching under my arms, and I won't be able to eat too much tonight as my pants feel like they've been spray-painted onto my body. Are white pants a good idea for a dinner date? If it were an ordinary date I'd have tried on five outfits by now and asked Peyton's advice, but obviously I can't do that tonight. Our argument has sliced the edge off my enthusiasm, which is *really* pissing me off because I was looking forward to my date. I was also excited about my new acting job, but all I can hear is Peyton accusing me of selling myself. How did we get here?

I hear the doorbell, followed by voices, then the sound of feet marching upstairs and finally, a door slam. I guess that Nate has arrived and Peyton has sent herself to her room to sulk. Good. She can stay there for a week, the miserable sack of spite.

I pick out a diamanté clutch bag and team it with strappy sandals. I already decided to wear my waist-length hair loose. It's my best feature by a mile, especially when I've straightened it and used half a can of shine serum. I give it one last brush through and head downstairs, but my phone pings en route.

JJ: Have a great night tonight, sis. Don't forget to use protection, I'm too young to be an uncle.

My god, he's such an idiot. As if my stomach didn't already feel like it was housing an entire planet full of nervous butterflies. Why does he have to make me feel ten times worse? I never get first-date nerves. Ever.

I text him back: *How dare you! I'm far too classy to put out on the first date.*

This, of course, is a lie. I've banged on a first date several times – which brings me some level of certainty that if I take a trip to the boneyard tonight, there mightn't be a repeat performance. In the case of Cooper, my co-worker at the Cosmic Diner, screwing him on a first date gave him the idea that

53

bombarding me with photos of his dick was a great move. Ugh. That's just what every girl wants to see on her phone, isn't it? Historically, I haven't cared if a guy had a rule that getting sex on a first date meant I wasn't worthy of a second date. If I've decided to have sex with a guy, it's because I *want* to have sex with a guy.

But Nate already feels different to everybody else, and I'm unsettled by that. Having anxiety about whether or not I'm good enough for a guy is just not me. I've always lived in the moment. I love my happy, chaotic, give-no-shits life because it gives me the power to let go and be free and just see where life takes me.

I march downstairs, throw off my self-doubts and bound confidently into the living room accompanied by a huge, fearless smile. I'm going to carpe the fuck out of this diem if it's the last thing I do.

Nate, dressed in a mulberry shirt and fitted black jeans, stands to greet me. Our eyes connect, his smile lights up the room, and my vagina starts drumming out a beat in preparation for tonight's totally inevitable party.

Jeez, I need to calm down. *I will not have sex tonight, I will not have sex tonight, I will not have sex tonight.* But why shouldn't I have sex tonight? I clearly *want* to have sex tonight, don't I? He's hot, I'm horny and does a bear crap in the woods? Is a frog's ass watertight?

Oh god, I'm screwed. I literally have zero self-restraint.

* * *

54

Nate has hired a chauffeur-driven Mercedes to take us to a secret location. I assume it's going to be a restaurant, but I can't think why it would be a secret one. I try to relax, but I'm still pissed off about Peyton. My mind keeps taking me back to our argument and how she put a complete downer on my movie news. I have no idea how we're going to dissolve the bad feelings.

As we head onto the Santa Monica Freeway, I sense Nate is feeling uneasy too. He clears his throat twice but doesn't say anything, then he starts fiddling with a cufflink.

"I need to apologise," I say just as he opens his mouth to speak.

"Oh. Why?" He looks anxious, like there's something on his mind that he doesn't want to share.

"For my mind being elsewhere, but it seems yours is too. Are you okay?"

"Yes," he says quickly, but the crackly edge to his voice betrays him. I smile as warmly as I can, until his own expression softens. "You're doing that thing again."

"What?"

"That thing where you know what I'm thinking without me having to tell you."

"Ah, that," I say with a laugh. "Yeah, I've been told I'm good at that. I'm good at other things too, like listening and giving advice. Do you want to share?"

His eyes shift away from me. "Something Richie said tonight is bothering me."

I feel my skin heat up, burning my cheeks. "Did

he say something about me?"

He nods. "Just that you and Peyton had an argument. I'm sorry you're fighting."

I exhale a deep breath. "There's no need for you to be sorry. Friends fight from time to time."

"No, you don't understand." He rests his elbow on the armrest of his seat and brings his hand to his chin. "I think this could be my fault. I have history with Peyton."

Bam! He doesn't need to say anything more. I know how this story ends – with me as a shitty friend who hasn't so much broken the girl code as stamped all over it. Has he made me the type of woman I hate? Am I out on a date with a man my best girlfriend has the hots for? I want to throw on the brakes. "I don't feel comfortable with this. You should have told me."

He sighs. "It didn't even occur to me"

I'm confused. "Wait, why not? Are you telling me you slept with my friend and didn't think it was worth mentioning?"

"No, that's not it," he says firmly, and for all my skills of intuition, I have no idea what he's talking about. "I only met Peyton once before, years ago, when I was in LA on business. She'd just got together with Richie, and Riley was a tiny baby. To cut a long story short, she came on to me, totally out of nowhere, and I said no. I thought that was that, but months later, she felt guilty enough to tell Richie all about it. You know what kind of guy he is. It took him weeks to call me up in London and confront me. I hadn't done anything wrong, but I still felt like shit. Richie's been my best mate for eleven years."

Oh god, why is Peyton like this? She has a knack for creating drama, but I never thought she'd be capable of doing something this crappy. "Thank you for telling me," I say softly. "I didn't know any of this, but I should have guessed. I admit fighting with Peyton has dampened my spirits a little tonight."

"What did she say to you?"

My heart sinks. "Peyton has a problem with a movie I'm doing, among other things. I don't want you to think this is all down to you."

"It sounds like she's jealous."

"And I can't do anything about that, so let's enjoy our night."

The car turns off the freeway and takes us towards Culver City. I look out of the window at the familiar boulevard lined with palm trees and flanked by multi-storey parking lots and Japanese car dealerships. My curiosity reaches peak excitement and . . . oh my god . . . is it? Richie must have told him. Boy, has this guy done his homework. I jerk forward in my seat. I can feel my pulse ringing in my ears. "Are you freaking kidding me?"

Nate laughs. "You seem happier."

Flecks of golden light from the amber sunset reflect in his dark eyes. I hold my breath as the car drives through the iron security gates and stops outside the stage door. The driver gets out and opens the door for us. My heart beats as fast as a hummingbird's as I take in my surroundings. This is already the best date I've ever had in my entire life. I want to bottle it and keep it forever.

Nate places his hand gently on my back as we

enter a building full of glass-walled offices. My skin shivers under his touch. We walk through a labyrinth of corridors, festooned with classic movie posters, until we find ourselves outdoors again.

"Welcome to Tara."

A guy dressed in navy blue butler's livery greets us amidst green poplar trees decorated with fairy lights, which trace their way up a path to the mansion used for Tara in *Gone with the Wind*. It's my absolute favourite film of all time. "*I can't think about that right now. If I do, I'll go crazy. I'll think about that tomorrow.*" Seriously, if I didn't have hardass Viking blood coursing through my veins, I'd want some of Scarlett O'Hara's. Well, except for the racism. And the selfishness. Okay, okay, I'll just take the courage, grit and glamour.

Nate takes my arm and we follow the fake butler to the fake mansion's veranda. We sit down on white chairs decorated with green velvet. Before us is a table set for dinner. There are flowers and fairy lights everywhere, making the setting magical on a scale of infinity.

"You arranged all this in one day?" I don't even try to hide how stunned I am.

"Not exactly," says Nate. His warm skin crinkles with the most beautiful grin. "I've been planning it since I first asked you out on Saturday morning. I wasn't certain you'd agree, of course. I only hoped. Then I interrogated Richie about your favourite things."

"Well, I'm very impressed."

The butler opens a bottle of champagne with a wonderful pop, and pours for us. Then he rolls out a trolley with our starters and announces the dish as potato soup with nettles.

I'm speechless. "How did you . . . I mean, nowhere in California cooks Danish cuisine."

Nate thanks the waiter then uncurls his napkin. "I know a guy who cooks," he says, as if uncovering my favourite food and finding someone to cook it is that simple. Maybe it is simple for him. I find myself wondering if he's richer and more influential than I thought. Like a younger, fitter English version of Bill Gates. But then another thought hits me. If Nate *is* rich enough to pull something like this off to impress a woman, why is he selling the theatre?

"How's your soup?" he asks.

The warm liquid slides down my throat and the flavours remind me of home: my family, Midsummer, sailing on the Baltic, ice skating at the Rådhuspladsen at Christmas, great times with great friends. "It's perfect."

"Do you miss Denmark?"

"Sometimes. I miss my dad. I haven't seen him since I moved out here – airfares are too expensive." He nods knowingly, but how can he know what it's like to be so cash-strapped you can't go home? "Did you miss England when you lived here?"

He shakes his head. "Not in the slightest. I appreciated every second of every day I was out here because I didn't know how long it would last." He pauses, his eyes lost in a memory. "I love LA."

"Then why don't you move back?"

A nerve in his jaw twitches. "It was always going to be short term. I'm a Klein and there are expectations . . ." He runs his spoon through his soup, resisting making eye contact with me. It's like every twist and turn is reflecting his inner turmoil.

"Richie said you have blue blood?"

"Only very distantly, through my mother. I think I'm like one hundredth in the line to the throne."

"Holy shit, you're kidding me!"

"Nope, not kidding," he says, beaming another gorgeous smile. "I'm just behind distant baby cousins I'll probably never meet and in front of a guy who owns a run-down castle in the Scottish Highlands. But I don't have a title or any wealth from my mother's side. By contrast, my father's power and influence is huge."

"Have you met the Queen?"

"Yeah, a couple of times," he says with a chuckle. I start to worry whether I'm too impressed by this. Do all posh English people know the Queen? Is it no big deal? "Her Majesty is a cousin twice – or is it three times? – removed."

I carefully pick my jaw up off my plate. "This is unreal."

His entire body smiles at me again. I feel his warmth radiate inside me like caged sunbeams, and I want to learn everything there is to know about this brilliant man and his family. We finish our starters and the waiters bring out a main course of poached salmon with langoustines on a bed of pickled fruit and vegetables. Nate tops up my glass for me.

"So, *Gone with the Wind*, eh? Where did that come from?"

"My mother." His eyes linger on me as I think back to my childhood in Copenhagen. We lived in a topsy-turvy house on the outskirts of the city, with views over the Øresund. The bedroom I shared with my sister was on the ground floor, the kitchen was in the middle, and our living room with a balcony and huge sliding doors was on the top floor. "She kinda indoctrinated me and my sister when we were tiny, but I grew to love the film even more than she did. We used to dress up in the white bridesmaids' dresses from our aunt's wedding, and our mother bought us green parasols and straw hats." I look around me at the house and let the fact I'm here with a gorgeous man who could give Rhett Butler a run for his money sink in. "If I still had that outfit, I'd be wearing the shit out of it right now."

He laughs. "I'd love to see that. Are you and your mum still close?"

Toxic memories invade my mind. I pour half a glass of white wine down my neck in an attempt to obliterate them. "No. I've seen her twice in the last ten years. She has a new family now."

"Ah, I'm sorry to hear that."

"Don't be," I say quickly. I don't want my date to turn into a pity party. "I was always closer to my dad."

"What does he do?"

"He's retired now, but he used to be a vet. He lives in a little wooden house in Christiana – which is a free-living hippy village – with a menagerie of patched-up animals, including a goose, and a dog with three legs." Nate's eyes almost pop out of his head. "You'll think he's crazy, and he is – he's brilliantly crazy. He rides a bicycle and he sails a boat and he paints and everyone knows him."

"He sounds amazing," says Nate. "I wish my father had a bit of crazy in him. He can be . . . quite difficult to love sometimes."

"What about your mom?"

"She passed away when I was twelve."

My heart sinks. "Oh, I'm so sorry."

His posture stiffens as he waves off my apology. He doesn't want to talk about her. "I'm closest to my brother, Sam. He's a straight-up rock-solid guy, and we'd literally take a bullet for each other." He shakes his head. "Dad hasn't always treated him well. Sam's a good accountant, but Dad values business acumen, aggression and killer instincts. He doesn't give a shit that Sam has more loyalty and decency than the rest of us combined. He only sees what's on the surface and not what's underneath."

I listen to him talk, but mostly I watch him talk. I hear the cynicism in his tone and notice how he sits with his shoulders slumped.

"So when are you going to tell Richie the real reason you want to sell the theatre?"

He looks up, his eyes connecting hard with mine. "Hmmm?"

I give him a knowing look. "I know you're not selling the theatre to prove your dedication to your father."

He sits back in his chair and takes a sip of wine. His dark eyes are downcast, but I can still see them sparkle even when he isn't looking at me. "How do you know?"

"I'm a good listener."

"But I haven't said anything."

I look straight at him until his eyes meet mine. "When I said I was a good listener, I wasn't talking about your words. People say so much more without realising it. I listened to your tone of voice, the variations in your accent, the non-verbal sounds you made when talking about your father, which were different than when you talked about your brother. Then there's body language, the way you're holding your head, what you're doing with your hands and the way you look at me when I ask you questions. I don't know why you're lying, but I *do* know."

I think my powers of perception have rendered him impressed more than terrified. He twists the stem of his wine glass between his fingers.

"You don't have to tell me, but you should tell Richie."

He nods sadly. "Okay, you're right, so here it is. I need the money because I have an opportunity to break away. I want to set up on my own. My brother knows, but I can't tell my father. If there was any other way . . ." He looks so overwhelmed I have to fight my instincts to get up and give him a hug. "The money I put into the theatre came from my mother's estate when I turned twenty-one. She'd want me to do this. I want it to be her legacy."

I blow out a breath in defeat. Now I understand. "There's no other way?"

He shakes his head. "If there were, I'd do it in a heartbeat."

"You still need to tell Richie."

"I will. I just didn't want to give him a pathetic sob story." His tone is sincere, and I'm left with no doubt that he hates being in this situation. "You're very easy to talk to."

"So I've heard."

We finish the evening with banana cake – my favourite – followed by coffee. We listen to music, we dance on the veranda and then we talk about movies. He is genuinely happy about my new acting role and then, when it's close to midnight he announces that his car has arrived to take me home.

Usually, by this point on a date, a guy will have made a move. There will have been innuendo or flirting, and I've even had a guy come right out with a blatant "Do you wanna fuck?" But it seems Nate is different, and it seems that makes him even sexier.

The drive back to Santa Monica only takes ten minutes. The chauffeur parks up outside our house, and I thank Nate for a lovely evening.

"I want to see you again," he says. The car is dark, the space inside only illuminated by a dim silver glow from the moon and a flickering street light. I can just about see the intensity in his eyes.

"I'd like that."

"Great, I'll give you a call and arrange something." He gets out of the car, walks around to my side and opens the door for me.

I walk up the path to my house. "I have college and the diner, and I start shooting my movie on Friday, but I'll do whatever I can to free up some time while you're here." My stomach rolls. It's as if I've just realised that he's only going to be in my life for a fleeting moment. "I've had a great night."

"Me too."

He takes my hands and holds them tight for what seems like forever. Then he closes the space between us, tilts his head and kisses me so softly that I feel every movement his mouth makes on mine reverberate around my body. I place my hands on his chest, lean in and kiss him back.

When we break free he reaches out and glides his fingers through my hair. "What do you want from life, Freja Larsen?"

"I want to live it."

"Yeah, I think I do too."

He walks back to the car, leaving me with his taste on my tongue and the certainty that I'm falling hard.

5

I'M SEEING NATE AGAIN TOMORROW night. He wants to celebrate my first day of filming with me. His lack of judgement about the movie eases the hint of anxiety Peyton awakened with her outburst. For the past three days, our date, including the fabulous kiss, has barely left my mind. This is a very good thing, but it's also a very bad and worrying thing because I've started counting the days until he has to return to London. The fact he's only supposed to be here for a month is taking a serious edge off my joy.

I've just finished my early morning shift at the Cosmic Diner, and I'm definitely looking forward to a couple of weeks' break from skating around in a skimpy dress, balancing pancakes and milkshakes on a tray. Videl, my boss, employs a huge cast of aspirational actors on minimum wage plus tips. Ungodly shift hours are written into our contracts in exchange for audition and filming leave. I always considered that a fair deal, but this week I've spent so many hours skating around tables that my body involuntarily glides along the sidewalk every time I walk home. Can you get motion sickness from roller-skating?

"Sis, this club sandwich isn't up to Rocky's standard. Should I have a word with him?"

"No, he's called Rocky for a reason. Say one word about his pastrami on rye and he'll kick the shit out of you."

JJ winces, brings his knees up and bangs them on

the melamine table. "Since when was he so violent?"

"He isn't. He just doesn't like you, remember?"

JJ looks genuinely stunned. "Why doesn't he like me?"

"Because of that *Toy Story* thing."

"What? Because I said it contained the biggest plot hole of any Disney movie in the history of all Disney movies?"

"You argued with him for an entire hour."

"So?" he says, screwing up his nose. "I was right. If Buzz Lightyear didn't know he was a toy, then he wouldn't freeze every time Andy came into the room. The entire premise of the movie is dumb."

There's no point arguing with him. JJ never knows when to quit. For him, being right is far more important than being considerate of other people's feelings. Rocky may be six foot four and built like a buffalo's back end, but he's remarkably sensitive.

"You're a lawyer, JJ. Other people's brains don't work like yours." I squint as I give him the once-over. "Speaking of being a lawyer, why have you come to lunch dressed as Pee-wee Herman?" He's wearing a tartan bowtie, suspenders and a pink short-sleeved shirt. How did he think that was a good look when he got dressed this morning? I must have told him a thousand times that you can't wear pink if you have orange hair.

"I have court this afternoon. I'm second chair on a pro bono case. Another one. Like I've been telling you for months, the partners hate me."

"You're lucky they let you work part-time and study in a totally unrelated field. You've pretty much told them you're leaving law to be a movie director the second you graduate, so what do you expect?"

"Yeah, yeah, I know." He takes another bite of his sandwich and a huge glob of mayo drops onto the front of his shirt. "Oh hell, that's all I need." He dabs the creamy sauce off his clothes with a napkin.

I sit down opposite JJ at the booth, my roller skates clunking against the metal table legs.

"So, why are you here?"

"Huh?" His eyes flit down to his sandwich. "I'm having lunch."

"You are, but the last time you dressed like my grandfather the day we buried him, you were worrying yourself sick thinking Aaron had endometrial cancer – despite not having a womb."

"He had all the same symptoms."

"No he didn't. He had a urinary tract infection."

"Shush!" he barks. "If he ever found out I told you he'd never forgive me!"

"He's not here," I say, my eyes growing wide. "And if he ever found out you thought he had a womb, he'd dump you."

"I never thought that . . . it's just . . . okay, so I learned not to consult the internet about cancer symptoms that day. That doesn't mean—"

"Your clothes mean you're fretting, so out with it. What's the matter?"

He wipes his bearded chin on his napkin. "I've got two grand in savings and Aaron thinks he'll be able to find ten. You don't have to do the movie."

"What has my movie got to do with anything?"

He takes one last bite of sandwich, then pushes his plate to one side. "I was talking with Richie and he's worried."

"Richie is *worried*?" I say with a snap. "Are you sure it wasn't Peyton?"

"No. I mean, yes, she thinks it's a bad decision too." He rests his elbows on the tabletop and places his chin in his hands. "If you tell me honestly that you're fine with doing *that* kind of movie, I'll back off, but—"

"I'm a woman who looks a certain way, who wants to be an actress. I've done sex scenes and nudity before. It's just what's expected."

"Not like this you haven't." He speaks loudly and firmly, as if he's addressing a witness on the stand. "I don't think it's going to be as easy as you think."

I'm about to raise my voice to tell him he has no idea how hard or easy it's going to be because he isn't a woman, but I remind myself he also isn't my enemy. And neither is Richie. "JJ, I value where your heart is, and I'm grateful you care, but I honestly don't have any worries about the movie."

"I can get the day off tomorrow and come with you for moral support."

"No, you can't."

"Why not? You said you don't have a problem, so . . ."

"I don't have a problem, but I might have a problem if you were there gawking at me."

"Um, Freja, hello, I'm your gay twin brother."

"You're not, you're a pain in my ass."

He looks at me as if he's staring straight into my soul. This is unusual for us; our friendship is exclusively built on drinking, partying and taking the piss out of each other. JJ doesn't do deep. "I care about you, and Richie cares about you. He'd never say this to you, but he's worried you might be doing something you don't want to do for him and he feels guilty."

"Even if Richie didn't have financial woes, I'd have still done the movie. It's not like half of LA hasn't seem my tits already, right?"

His eyes seem to relax. "Okay," he says with a nod, but he's only half smiling.

"Is there anything else?"

"Hmm? Oh . . ." He takes a sip of his coffee and screws up his nose. "Your coffee is bad today too." He looks at his watch. "I need to get to court, but Aaron said he'd call me at twelve and he hasn't. I need to talk to him." His ginger eyebrows bend into a huge frown that crinkles his forehead.

"Jeez, JJ, he's only in a meeting. You'd think he was selling his soul to the devil."

His head snaps up. "That's exactly what he's doing."

"What do you mean?"

"When Richie first put Aaron in touch with Nate, I thought it was a great move, but his father . . . I wouldn't trust him as far as I could throw him. Aaron's life has revolved around getting 'Dave' on the market for years. The whole time he was working for Google in Silicon Valley he was obsessed with his virtual home assistant idea. From the first day I met him, it was all he thought about. I used to joke there were three guys in our relationship." JJ starts to laugh, but he can't hide how concerned he is. "A few days ago Joyco's stock market value dropped. They're contracted to Pixelate to make all of Dave's components for the next five years, so with their stock crashing, Klein & Co want to reduce their offer to buy Aaron's IP on the device. It's just that . . . I've found out Joyco's stock was deliberately shorted by traders who are connected to Klein."

"You're kidding?" My stomach plummets through the floor. Did Nate do this? Was he screwing over my best friend's boyfriend at the same time he was pursuing me with dates and flowers and hours-long phone calls? I swivel around in the booth, bend down and start to unlace my skates.

"Apparently Klein & Co has a track record for shorting stock to cut the best deals in buyouts. Aaron doesn't know about it yet and I can't reach him. He's been in a meeting with them since eight a.m. I arranged for a guy from my firm to act for him, but I can't reach him either. I've been calling both of them all morning. Klein & Co are a bunch of sharks while Aaron is phytoplankton. They'll be eating him alive."

"Leave it with me." My head is full of steam. How could he do this? Was this his plan all along? Was I just a distraction?

"What are you going to do?"

I stand and pick up my skates. "I'm going down there. If Aaron calls you after I'm gone, let me know straight away. They're not getting away with this."

* * *

I practically run up Santa Monica Boulevard, then I

take a bus to Beverly Hills. It takes forty minutes, and with no word from JJ, I realise the responsibility for saving Aaron's dream lies solely with me. Pixelate, the company Aaron set up when he left his graduate job in Silicon Valley, employs ten people and only started to turn a profit a few months ago.

The Klein family and their entourage of sharks would have to be staying at the Beverly Wilshire, wouldn't they? I didn't have time to change, so when I walk into the lavish hotel, I'm still wearing my blue waitress uniform, teamed with white sneakers and a sloppy grey cardigan.

Dozens of pairs of eyes belonging to beautiful people dressed in clothes it would take me a year to pay for fall upon me as I strut purposefully through the hotel lobby. If Hollywood has a remake of *Pretty Woman* in the pipeline, then whoever they've cast to play Julia Roberts's role better start worrying. I might not be wearing thigh-high boots, but my short, too-much-information waitress dress appears to be giving off a definite Sunset Strip vibe.

"Miss, can I help you?" A huge black guy in navy security uniform appears like a brick wall in front of me. Crap, am I not allowed inside? Does he think I'm a hooker? Should I start running? *Tænk, Freja. Tænk! Think!*

"Hi, I work for Pixelate. I need to speak to my colleague immediately."

The security guy looks me over, his eyes lingering on my bare legs. "You work for who?"

"Pixelate. They're having a meeting somewhere in this hotel. I've just come from Brockman & Barnes, Pixelate's lawyers, and I need to see

72

Aaron— um, Mr Goodwin as a matter of urgency. Call through to him if you have to. Tell him Freja Larsen is here to see him."

The security guy walks over to talk to the receptionist at the front desk. The immaculately dressed woman looks at me, shrugs, reads something off a monitor, then looks over at me one more time. Finally, the security guy returns. "They're in the Chateau Room."

Yes! My god, I'm good.

I follow directions which lead me past marble-tiled hallways lit by decadent chandeliers. The historic hotel oozes Hollywood glamour, with huge vases full of red roses, glossy art deco-style furniture and dramatic archways that look like they belong in a Venetian palace. The rubber soles of my sneakers squeak on the polished floor, and I wish I'd taken twenty minutes to go home and change my clothes. I look like I should be pushing a vacuum around the hotel's rooms.

When I reach the Chateau Room, I can hear voices from behind the walnut double doors. My pulse speeds up and my gut churns, not because of what I have to do, but because Nate is inside the room.

I reach out to knock on the door, but before I do, it swings open and a smartly dressed young woman with gorgeous light-brown skin and long dark hair edges her way outside. "Hi," she says in a low voice. She offers me her hand to shake. "I'm Sandy. It's Freja, isn't it? How can I help you?"

"You knew I was here?"

"Yes, the receptionist just called up."

"Well, Sandy, they should have told you I

wanted to see Aaron. Is he in there?"

"They did tell us, but he's very busy at the moment." Sandy has a kind smile, but her huge dark eyes, which are framed by the longest, thickest lashes I think I've ever seen, reveal timidity. "I'm Lord Klein's international assistant. He asked me to speak with you."

Clearly, Sandy has been given gatekeeping orders. "Look, Sandy, with all due respect, Aaron is one of my closest friends. I came here to see him and I'm not leaving until I do."

Sandy's full lips fill her thin face in an awkward smile. "Then watch how you go."

Her words, and the frailty with which she says them, make my skin goosebump. "Is that some kind of threat?"

She shakes her head weakly. "No, it's just friendly advice."

I hesitate for a moment, then I place my hand on the door handle. What on earth am I about to walk into? A scene from *The Godfather*? I push the weirdness out of my mind and walk into the room.

And I find myself in a scene from *The Godfather*.

Aaron and a man I assume is JJ's lawyer friend sit on one side of a long table. On the other side there's a young man in a dark suit, then a very old man in a dark suit, then a couple of spare seats, then at the head of the table sits Don fucking Klein himself.

Dark-brown eyes, embedded in a weathered but distinguished face, bore into me ferociously. I suck in a sharp breath, but I manage to keep my shoulders straight and my head high. He's wearing

74

a dark suit, just like the other two men, and he has receding dark-grey hair and a wiry beard that hugs his long chin. He has the same eyes and the same warm skin tone as Nate, but while Nate's beautiful smiling eyes emit sunshine, his father's cold, hard stare could wilt daisies.

"Miss Groza," Klein barks at Sandy, who is standing next to me, "I thought I told you to deal with this interruption."

Sandy looks petrified, so I step forward. "I need to speak to my friend. It will only take a minute."

Aaron stands up. "Is it serious? Has anything happened to JJ?"

"No, he's fine. I've just had lunch with him—"

"Freja?"

I spin around quickly at the sound of Nate's voice. He looks between me and his father, then he looks at the beautiful woman with long golden hair who currently has her arm threaded through his. When his gaze returns to me, his eyes are clouded with guilt.

"Who is this girl, Nate?" the woman says in a plummy English accent, tightening her hold on Nate's arm. As she looks down her long nose at me, I can't help but notice that her face seems to be no stranger to plastic surgery. Her skin has a healthy glow, but her red mouth has an odd, unnatural shape. And I swear to god, if she's his girlfriend, or his fiancée, or his fucking wife, then I'll go for his throat.

"This is Freja. She's a friend of Richie's." Nate's Adam's apple bobs against his shirt collar. Who the hell is this woman and why is he friend-zoning me? Is he ashamed of me?

"I'm also the girl Nate is dating." Does one incredible date and the promise of another count as "dating"? Probably not, but I don't give a shit.

"You're dating a *waitress*?" Lord Klein's voice booms into the room. He makes zero effort to disguise how outraged he is. "Not again, Nathaniel. Please tell me you're not messing around with a waitress." His eyes trace the entire length of my body. "Or is she a trailer-park stripper?"

Åh min Gud! I take another step forward, slightly appalled that none of the men in the room, including Aaron, are leaping to my defence. "You care to repeat that?"

The young man sitting closest to me, who I'm guessing is Nate's brother, shrinks in his seat. The old man next to him clears his throat nervously. Are they all afraid of him?

"Freja, maybe we should talk outside."

"Oh, we *will* be talking, Nate. I promise you that. But I came here to speak to Aaron, nobody else."

Aaron gets out of his seat. "Sit down," barks Lord Klein, and in a move that makes me want to grab Aaron by his shoulders and shake the living daylights out of him, he does as he's told. "I'm doing business here, girl. Nobody interrupts my meetings."

Lord Klein is clearly a man who has used power and privilege to get exactly what he wants for a very long time. Men like Lord Klein don't move in the same circles as I do. He knows nothing about me, but he took one look at my waitress uniform and decided I deserved to be spoken to as if I were a piece of dog crap stuck to the sole of his Italian leather shoes. Unlike everyone else in the room, that's not something I'm going to lie down and take.

"You're still here?" says Lord Klein.

"I *am* still here," I say, meeting a glare I know is aimed to intimidate. "I'm not going anywhere until I've spoken to Aaron."

I feel Nate take my elbow. When did the blonde let go of him? "Come on, Freja. Surely it can wait."

"No, actually, it can't." I shrink out of his hold. He bites his lip and looks nervously around the room. Do I know him even half as much as I thought I did? I soon realise I have a clear choice to make. On one side are JJ and Aaron, my friends; on the other is Nate, a guy I have the hots for. I stare into Nate's gorgeous dark eyes, searching for something . . . anything. "Did you know?"

He buries his hands in his pockets. "Know what?"

"That your father paid people to short Joyco's stock so he could reduce Aaron's buyout?"

His face darkens, but his eyes don't leave mine. He locks his jaw and a nerve pulses in his cheek. I can hear the sound of his breaths leaving his body, but I don't know if he's angry at me, or his father. "No, I didn't know."

"You'd better have evidence to prove all of this, young lady." Lord Klein stands and rests his body weight on the table with his fists. "If you don't, I'll sue you for defamation."

"Sue me. I have nothing to give you if I lose." If Lord Klein thinks he can threaten me with self-entitled bluster, he has another thing coming. I ignore him and talk directly to Aaron. "JJ was waiting for you to call him. He'd be here himself, but he had court this afternoon. I promised I wouldn't let you be cheated."

Aaron hates any kind of confrontation. He's a quiet soul and a people pleaser. "I should talk it all through with JJ, I guess."

Lord Klein shuffles some papers into a pile in front of him. His skin is as red as a snapping lobster. "Leave the room now and the entire deal is off."

"No, it isn't." Nate steps forward and faces his father, their steely gazes concentrated on each other. "If Aaron needs extra time to look over our contract, he's got it."

I expect Lord Klein to be beyond angry, but I spot a faint trace of a smile. "Are you speaking as Klein & Co's new managing director?"

Nate stands tall, his shoulders straight. "I am."

Aaron and his lawyer get up from the table and politely inform the others that they'll be in touch by the end of the week. Aaron looks like a rabbit who got caught in nuclear-power-fuelled headlights. I follow them both out into the bright hallway.

"Freja, wait!" Nate calls.

I tell Aaron I'll be a minute, and I let Nate catch up.

"I promise I didn't know, and I'll get to the bottom of it."

"We're already at the bottom of it, Nate. You must know this is who your father is."

"I'm sorry he spoke to you like that."

"Are you?"

He bristles. "Of course I am. He had no right."

"You should have challenged him on how he spoke to me. What did he call me again? A trailer-park stripper?" I let out a laugh as if that will shake off how pissed I am. "I think your family is waiting for you." I walk away from him. I've never felt like such a misfit before. These people aren't my tribe. I can't and won't fit with people like this and I don't even want to try.

"Wait." He catches up with me again. "What about tomorrow night?"

"Are you kidding?"

"No. No, I'm not." His dark eyes glisten and he swallows hard. I immediately feel bad about writing him off. It isn't his fault that his father is a megalomaniac. But then I remember the blonde. "Who's the woman you were with?"

"Her name's Evelyn. We grew up together. She's a widow, I'm godfather to her kids, and she came out here with her father." He points his thumb in the direction of the meeting room. "Her father is Sir Cuthbert Ashby, Dad's business partner and the 'Co' in Klein & Co."

"Have you ever slept with her?"

"No. As I said, we all grew up together: the Kleins and the Ashbys."

He isn't lying – I'd know if he was. "Okay. Fine." I turn to walk away from him.

"So, are we still on for tomorrow?"

"I'll think about it."

6

TWILIGHT STUDIOS BEGAN LIFE IN the eighties and specialised in shooting pop music videos and commercials. Then, sometime after the millennium, it began to make the kind of made-for-TV movies you could only watch if you paid a hefty subscription fee to premium sexy but "not porn" cable channels.

Twisted Street is one of those movies, and it has already been purchased by one of those channels.

I arrive on set early and I'm immediately shown to my trailer. I haven't had my very own trailer since I played Inga in Scandi noir police series, *Den Store Løgn*, three years ago. And this trailer is nice. I have a small kitchen area, a seating area, a shower and, at the back, there's a room with a double bed that almost touches the walls on both sides. I'm feeling quite important and very pleased with myself.

What makes today even better is the huge bouquet of pink and gold daisies, roses and peonies that is waiting for me. I assume they're from Reed, or the studio, but when I pick out the card it says *Knock 'em dead. Nate.* And I enter into a state of elation which can only be described as a giddy swoon. Ugh. Evidently, he's still solidly under my skin.

JJ was thankful I helped Aaron out of a near-catastrophic business deal with Lord Klein –

hereafter renamed Darth Klein – yesterday. He wanted to take a sick day so he could "chaperone" me, but I told him he was being ridiculous. Seriously, if I've told him once, I've told him a thousand times, I'm totally cool with being butt-naked in front of a film crew. Why wouldn't I be? My friends have all heard about my dad's legendary Midsummer parties. We'd bring a feast out onto our boat and go skinny-dipping in the canals. My dad – who turns sixty-five next year – is always the first to strip off and dive in.

Today, we're filming the sex scene on a kitchen counter. It's the first time my character, Maya, gets it on with Todd Warner's character, Drew. For reasons best known to the woman who wrote *Twisted Street*, Maya keeps her panties, stockings, suspenders and six-inch high heels on while she and Drew devour each other.

I'm due in make-up in twenty minutes, so I strip to my shorts and tank top and cover myself with a loose cotton robe. There's a knock at my door. I assume it's going to be a member of the film crew, but it's Todd Warner, dressed in jeans and an orange t-shirt.

"Hi, it's Freja, right?" he says from behind a pair of jet-black sunglasses. I used to watch Todd on an NBC medical show called *On Call*. He played Hanson, a hot paramedic with bipolar disorder. I always thought he was good-looking in a non-sexy, squeaky-clean, boy-next-door kinda way, but he looks much older in the flesh. His skin is so rough it looks like it's been rubbed with salt and deep fried. "I just thought I'd drop by to say hi before we start shooting today."

"Oh, yeah, hi. Do you want to come in?"

Todd climbs the steps and follows me inside my trailer. He removes his glasses to reveal startling turquoise eyes, then he sits down on the padded sofa-seat and crosses his legs. Then he uncrosses them. Then he re-crosses them again. Well, isn't this a turn up? It seems hot, experienced actor Todd is quite literally terrified.

"Can I get you a drink?"

Todd clears his throat and coughs. "Water would be great."

"I hope I have some." I look around the little kitchen, which consists of four low cupboards, one of which has a stovetop, and four wall cupboards. Which one is the refrigerator? I open the door to the first cupboard on the left and find it stocked with six bottles of mineral water. "Ah-ha, we're in luck." I pour the water into a glass for him.

"So, Reed says you're a student?" Todd has a huge drink and his body starts to relax.

"Yes. I'm studying for a master's in film production at UCLA. While also waiting tables and trying to be an actress." I sit down on a wooden chair opposite him. "I used to watch *On Call* when I first moved to the States. That was before it jumped the shark with that crazy ménage-a-trois plotline."

Todd laughs. "Oh god, don't remind me. Thankfully they killed off poor old Hanson before that storyline aired. I'm pleased I missed all the fan drama. I'm good friends with some of the cast. Two of the guys got death threats over it."

"Oh my god, really?"

"Yeah," he says, twisting his bottom lip. "It's scary how obsessed people can get with TV characters. It's like once you're invited into their living rooms, they feel they're personally connected to you – like you're their friend or, sometimes, their lover. I've had women mail me marriage proposals."

"Oh, jeez. That's worse than weird." A chill runs down my spine when I imagine some guy watching Maya's sex scenes and "feeling" a personal connection to her. Ew. I wish Todd hadn't put that thought in my head, but at least it's broken the ice. At least, it has for me. Todd is struggling to make eye contact and sweating through his shirt.

"So, I guess this is a bit of an unusual film we've signed up for." Todd's gaze flicks to me for the briefest of seconds before returning to his glass.

"Have you done this kind of role before?" I ask him.

He shakes his head. Christ almighty! I was expecting him to reel off a catalogue of acting jobs that have required him to at least take his shirt off. He's toned and tanned with a square jaw and a pretty face. He must be every woman's vision of an all-American hero. "This is my first time. I'm a little embarrassed to admit that at my age."

"I remember my first time. I needed five full nights of friend therapy, and I didn't eat for days." He smiles at me, but he still looks petrified. "And I drank a *lot* of alcohol."

"To be honest, I thought I could do this, but now that the day has arrived, I'm totally freaking out. I came here hoping with everything I had that you'd be unattractive, but . . . well, you're not. Sorry, I shouldn't have said that. I hope you don't mind."

I laugh. "Not at all."

Finally his eyes connect with mine. "So, how many times have you done this?"

"A few times," I say reassuringly. "I don't think any actress finds sex scenes easy, but it's far worse if you're repulsed by the person you have to act with. This one time, when I was still a teenager, I had to pretend to give one of Denmark's most famous and almost seventy-year-old actors a blow job. I needed the stiffest of drinks to get through it."

"Oh god." He looks genuinely offended for me. "Yeah, it could definitely be a lot worse."

"It could, but you just need to switch off and remind yourself it isn't real."

"I've always avoided these kinds of roles. I've kissed actresses, obviously, but they've always been, um, clothed." He shifts awkwardly in his seat again, his fingers playing with the rubber edging of the table. "I'm just coming out of a ten-year relationship. I signed up for this to relaunch my career, and between you and me, it's probably an early midlife crisis thing too. But I want to do everything I can to make you feel relaxed. Once we're filming, if you're not comfortable with how I'm holding you or if I'm touching you, um, wrong, then promise you'll tell me straight away?"

"I promise. As long as *you* promise to stop overthinking this." I offer him my hand so we can shake on the deal.

"I'll try my best." He smiles and flashes the brightest whitest teeth I've ever seen. "I'm sorry we have to get straight into it this morning. I'd have liked some rehearsal time, you know, to make it less weird."

"Did you get to rehearse with the previous

actress before she bailed?"

"No, Anna left on the first day. I've shot almost all of my scenes with Julia Bowman already, but with Anna there were some difficulties from the start . . . and that brings me nicely on to the other thing I came here to say." He finishes his water and stands up. "I'm due in costume in five, but to get straight to the point, Reed can be a bit of a jerk. It's like he's been picked up from a Texas ranch in the seventies and dropped in Hollywood without anybody telling him the world has changed."

I've suffered through hours of the man's lectures, so I can imagine. "Did Anna walk because of Reed?"

"Let's just say Anna had a low threshold for Reed's demands."

Åh Gud. What have I let myself in for?

"Thanks for the warning." I join Todd at the door and open it for him. "I think I'll be able to handle him."

* * *

Christy Lederer is in charge of costume and make-up for *Twisted Street*. She welcomes me to the make-up room with a cup of steaming hot coffee and a pile of trashy gossip magazines.

"You're wearing panties, heels and stockings in this scene," she says, flipping through the shooting schedule. "And a bra . . . briefly. Okay, I got these to fit Anna, but you're roughly the same size." She passes me a pair of purple satin panties and a matching bra. "Your cup size is smaller than

85

Anna's, so if it doesn't fit I'll have to call Victoria's Secret and get a replacement couriered out."

I take off my robe and put on the underwear. The bra is a D, and I'm a C, but Anna must have a narrower back as it seems to fit perfectly on the tightest fastening.

Christy looks me over, adjusting the bra straps and fiddling with the material. "You need an all-over body tint."

"A what?"

She wheels out a plastic trolley with three drawers from the corner of the room. "A body tint. Your skin is too pale. You'll look like a corpse under the studio lights."

"Oh, I see. How long will it take?"

"Not long. I just spray it on you and rub it in." She chuckles softly. "Don't worry. In the scenes where you're dead, we can skip it."

I have a premonition – a nightmarish one. "This won't make me orange, will it? I can't go near spray tans, you know, given my hair." When I was seventeen, my best friend, Agnes, coerced me into getting a spray tan with her for our school prom. I looked like a Cheeto.

Christy chews the inside of her mouth. "Trust me. I'm a pro." This is easy for her to say. With her mass of dark-brown curls and light-brown skin tone, she's never had this worry. "I'll try you with a zero-two, which is the palest I have."

"How pale is it?"

"Darker than white, lighter than . . ." She compares the zero-two with the zero-four. "Yes, this one is more porcelain than peach. Give me your arm and I'll test it."

I do as she says, she decides it looks fine, and she starts to spray the tinted lotion all over my body. I realise this will be happening every day now, and my body responds with a gigantic yawn. It never occurred to the make-up people in Denmark that I should have a tan, but that's California for you.

It takes twenty minutes for Christy to make my translucent skin look alive. "You've been drafted in at short notice," she says. "How'd you find learning all your lines?"

"Fine, but I don't have too many lines."

"Ah, right." Christy gives me a knowing look. "This stuff needs to dry, so don't put your robe back on for a couple of minutes."

"Can I sit down?" I'm standing in the middle of the room with my legs apart and my arms positioned so I'm not touching my body. The room is too warm and I feel like my fake tan is starting to melt.

She shakes her head. "Sorry, honey. Your ass needs to dry too."

"Now there's a sentence I didn't expect to hear . . . ever . . . in my entire life."

Christy gives a throaty chuckle. "Well, you *did* choose this line of work."

"I was called to the stage," I say jokily. "I don't think I was called to stand stark bollock naked while a stranger sprays something that looks and smells like PAM cooking oil all over my intimate parts."

A huge smile spreads over Christy's face. She's sweet. I like her. "Yes, there are certainly more comfortable ways to spend a Friday morning. How are you feeling about the role?"

"I'm totally fine," I say for the millionth time.

"Think of it this way," says Christy. "When you walk onto that set, you'll instantly become the most powerful person in this entire studio because nobody else is prepared to do what you're going to do. You need to own it and be proud of how brave you are."

Jeez, I think that's the nicest thing anyone has ever said to me. I swallow a lump in my throat. "Thanks, Christy. That means a lot."

"You're welcome. I sure as hell know I couldn't do it. But then I have a few too many jiggly bits. I'd kill for your figure."

I feel guilty for all the exercise sessions I haven't done and all the salads I haven't eaten in the past decade. "I was blessed with great genes," I say honestly as Christy pulls lipsticks, eye shadows and an array of brushes out of her trolley. "I'd also be lying if I said I wasn't nervous, but I had a little chat with Todd earlier and he made me feel much better. Not least because he's way more nervous than me."

"Todd is such a sweet guy," she says with a sigh. "His career flatlined after he was sacked from *On Call*. Then his wife left him. Poor guy really needs this movie. Reed needs it too. His ass has been on the line since day one, and don't we all know it."

There's something in her tone that sends shivers down my spine. "What do you mean?"

"Well you know Anna, your predecessor, walked off the set, right?" She prods my arms, then looks to see if any colour has come off onto her fingers. "I think you're cooked. You can sit." I put the purple panties back on and sit down in a grey swivel chair. "Anna and Reed had a difference of opinion over Maya's pubic hair."

Woah! I wasn't expecting that. "Please tell me Reed isn't pro-bush, because if he is, it's a little late to be having this conversation. I spent a good hour in the waxing salon yesterday."

"No, but Anna *was* pro-bush and she refused to comply," Christy recalls with a shudder. "Reed went apeshit when I told him."

I'm not sure I blame him. I'd hazard a guess that the "apeshit" part will have been totally unnecessary, but Anna sounds unprofessional. A quick bikini wax isn't as big a deal as standing naked in a baking hot room while somebody covers you from head to toe in peachy-porcelain gunk.

The door to the make-up room suddenly slams open and Reed barges in. For crying out loud, didn't anybody ever teach him to knock first? He stares at me for a moment, then looks over at Christy, who passes me my robe. "I need her on set in five. Do something with her nipples. They need to be darker."

And then he's gone.

If I'd ever had cause to wonder what it would feel like to be treated like a slab of meat, now I know.

* * *

I wish I had a dollar for every time Todd has asked me if I'm okay. Every time he has to grab my ass, or rip his shirt off, or kiss me, or lick whipped

89

cream off my stomach, he's checked with me first. He is as considerate as Reed is offensive. Clearly, nobody has ever put Reed McHale on a course about sensitive language in the workplace. When he's not talking about my tits, ass or pussy, he's mentioning Todd's cock or dropping c-bombs in all the wrong places. Todd told me he'd been plucked from a seventies Texan ranch. I think it's fairer to say he's been plucked from a seventies porn store, after he was loaned the mind and soul of Larry Flynt.

"Todd," Reed says, "you need to get Freja's bra off in the next take, and Freja, I want to see Todd's butt after he lifts you back onto the kitchen counter. Leave his cock in his pants, I just want his ass on camera." An older crew member called Miguel manoeuvres a camera onto a dolly grip and waits for the go-ahead. "When you get her bra off, grab hold of one of her tits and suck it."

Todd turns bright red and freezes. His hands are planted on my hips and I can feel his pulse through his quivering palms. "It's fine. You'll be fine," I say to him, while trying very hard to mentally dismiss Reed's awfulness. The man has the nurturing skills of a snake.

"I don't think . . . I can," stammers Todd. A scary-looking nervous vein pops out, tracing a snake-like pattern down the side of his head. "I'm so sorry."

"And action."

Nothing.

"Can we take a minute?" I ask. I'm suddenly terrified that Todd might be about to have a heart attack. Or some nervous-vein-related aneurism.

Reed looks at his watch. "We can break in ten. I need to get this scene out of the way. Come on now, Todd. Show me what you're made of."

Todd breathes hard. "Shit, I can't. This is bullshit."

"Close your eyes and imagine you're somewhere else," I tell him. "Is there a celebrity, or a model, anybody you're really horny for?"

Todd swallows so hard that his entire body tightens. His eyes sink under his brows. "That won't help. In fact, it'll make things worse. I don't have a problem getting into it. I'm worrying about getting into it *too* damn much."

Jesus Christ, please don't let him get a boner. I don't think he'd ever recover. "Erm . . . okay. Well, if something happens down in that area, don't worry about it. It's cool. I'll take it as confirmation I'm an awesome actress."

Miguel, who has the kindest, most soulful eyes I've ever seen, climbs back onto his camera dolly and gets ready. A grey-haired woman belted into jeans that are far too big around her middle places a clapperboard in front of the camera as Reed calls, "Action."

Todd's grip strengthens on my hips, then he says sorry for the thousandth time and kisses me.

I immediately get into character, flicking my head back to give Todd access to my neck, while grabbing fistfuls of his hair and desperately hoping with everything I have that he manages to keep his penis under control.

Out of the corner of my eye, I see the camera moving down the grip towards me as Todd's hands fumble around my back. Christy has already "fixed" the bra to make it easier for him to get off. I start praying again. Suddenly I feel the garment release and I shimmy out of the straps.

Then nothing.

"Fuck," Todd says.

"What the fuck do you mean by 'fuck'?" roars Reed. "Just grab hold of her tit."

Todd's hand moves through the air towards my left boob, but then it freezes. He looks like he's about to ring a doorbell.

Reed throws the script he's holding to the ground. "Are you fucking kidding me? Do you know how behind schedule this movie is? I don't have time for this. The only person doing her fucking job around here is Freja. If you can't touch her tit, then how the hell are you going to touch her pussy next week?"

Oh Christ, that's it. I've had enough. "This isn't helping," I say sharply, causing Reed's eyebrows to shoot up to meet his sweaty, wiry hairline. "Using that kind of language isn't going to help Todd's performance."

"The only thing that'll help his performance is if a fucking real man shows him how to touch a woman."

Todd bangs his fist on the wall behind me with an almighty thud. The set shakes and a picture frame crashes to the ground. "Damn it. I'm sorry."

"How do you expect him to get through this when you talk like that?"

Reed puffs out his chest. "You think you know more about directing movies than me, do you, sugar?" He walks towards me, his derisive gaze taking in the full length of my body. "You're a two-bit waitress who'll strip for a dime. Never forget what you are."

His words jangle around in my brain like razor-sharp daggers. I think back to how he recruited me in the lecture room just a few days ago – how didn't I see through his flattery? Todd gently grips my arm as if to keep me grounded, but a fire rises inside me and the only way to put it out is to let it out.

"How dare you?" I pull away from Todd and stand in front of Reed with my shoulders straight, trying to block out the fact that I'm half naked. I think back to Christy's words about being the most powerful person on this set, and although my voice is shaking even more violently than my body, I hold my head high. "Your neck was on the line when you came to me to do this film, and Todd is the best actor you can afford. You need to start talking to us with the respect we deserve, because if you don't, so help me god, I will walk off this set right now. You need us more than we need you, so learn some damn manners."

I walk away from him, pick up my robe and wrap it around my body. "We're taking a break right now. I'll be back in twenty minutes. *If* I've calmed down by then."

I hear Reed mutter a disgruntled "Who the hell does she think she is?" to the film crew as I march to my trailer and slam the door behind me.

7

IT'S ALMOST NINE P.M. WHEN I finish shooting. Reed apologised for his behaviour, Todd managed to get it together, and I did what was necessary, but spending close to ten hours shooting one scene was emotionally and physically gruelling. I feel like I could sleep for a week. Every bone in my body aches: my neck, my back, my arms – I even have twinges in the balls of my feet. An eight-hour shift at the diner is a walk in the park compared to this.

I shower in my trailer and get dressed in a pair of leggings and a loose yoga top. I can't say I'm completely happy with my performance today. I don't think I did my best work, because – stupidly – I let Reed McHale get to me. The way he spoke to me, and what he said, got under my skin and festered for the rest of the day. I look in the mirror and stare my reflection straight in the eye: *Stop it, Freja. You don't let someone who doesn't know you drag you down.*

Insecurity is something I battled, and won, when I was a kid. For more years than I dare to admit, I let my mother's desertion reflect on how I viewed myself. Maybe I didn't have a mother because she thought I didn't need her. I was too headstrong; I was too independent; I was too goddamn stubborn. Why else would she have left me? My sister and I blamed each other. Both of us felt our loss so deeply and so personally that we couldn't talk about it, so we tore ourselves apart, fighting each other's words with worse ones, until our dad packed us both off to therapy.

I was fifteen when I learned how to project confidence. I was sixteen when I learned to believe in myself. And I was seventeen when I vowed I'd never let anybody make me doubt who I am ever again. But then today happened and for a moment I was that scared little girl again, convinced I wasn't good enough. Is this all I'm good for? Am I selling myself? Does getting paid to take my clothes off make me trash? What do Richie and JJ *really* think about me doing this? What does Nate think?

I texted Nate to let him know that I had to work late. He said he'd booked a table at a restaurant close to Twilight Studios for nine thirty, but as the minutes ticked by, I sent him another text asking if we could rearrange. He agreed, but I feel so deflated. A big part of me is desperate to see him. And it isn't the vagina part of me this time. After spending all day simulating sex with a guy who was terrified to touch my boobs, I'm definitely not thinking with my vagina. But this means I'm thinking with my heart, which is a million times scarier.

I take a taxi home, hoping to crawl into bed as soon as I walk through my front door, but as we drive into my cul-de-sac I notice a familiar black Mercedes parked outside my house. My heart starts to race, but then I panic because I look like a drowned rat. My hair is still damp, I'm not wearing any make-up and I'm dressed like I'm one bounced paycheck away from sleeping on the streets. And it bothers me that I'm caring about stuff like this.

I pay the driver and get out of the cab. Nate gets out of his chauffeur-driven rental at exactly the same time and pulls a huge bouquet from behind his back.

"More flowers?" I tuck a clump of wet hair behind my ear.

"A girl can never have too many flowers," says Nate, handing them to me.

"Thank you. They're lovely." I inhale the fragrance: lilies, peonies and gorgeous sunshine-yellow daisies – my favourite.

"I really wanted to see you, and I couldn't wait until tomorrow." He pushes his hands deep into his pockets and smiles until his brow crinkles. "I hope you don't mind."

"I don't, except I look like I've had a fight with a hurricane and lost." I re-tuck the annoying clump of hair behind my ear.

"You look beautiful."

Jesus Christ, I swear my womb has just folded in on itself. "Thank you," I say again.

"I'll let you go now. Unless . . . you'd like to go somewhere?"

I look down at my clothes and worry about my hair some more. "I'm not really dressed for a date."

"Sure, you are. We'll have to ditch the fancy restaurant, but I have an even better idea. Come on." He opens the car door for me and I get inside.

Nate's chauffeur takes us the short distance to Santa Monica Pier. The spring night air feels wonderful as we stroll, arm in arm, along the famous boardwalk towards the Pacific Park funfair. It's a Friday night, so the fair is teeming with locals and tourists all set for a great night out. We pass restaurants, games arcades, and carts selling hats, sunglasses, cotton candy and hot dogs. The ocean breeze makes the palm trees rustle and the waves swish along the beach.

"Are you hungry?" he asks as we approach a hot dog cart.

"Oh my god!" I stop dead in my tracks. "This has never happened before. Well, not since I ate fermented herring at New Year's and got food poisoning for five days. I didn't realise, but I haven't eaten a thing all day."

"You're kidding." Nate laughs from deep in his chest. It's a delicious laugh that makes me want to throw my arms around his neck and kiss him. I'm a lost cause.

We order two hot dogs, two sodas, and some fries to share, then we sit down at a wooden picnic table opposite a funnel cake shop. We make small talk as we eat. Nate tells me all about the three years he lived with Richie in downtown LA, and I tell him about Denmark.

"So how do I say 'hello' in Danish?" he asks enthusiastically.

"You're going to be disappointed on that one. It's just 'hallo'."

He repeats 'hallo', replacing his clear English accent with a soft Scandinavian lilt.

"Now, I know I do not sound like that, Mr Klein," I say, affecting near-perfect Queen's English.

"Wow!" he says, dipping a fry in ketchup and popping it into his mouth. "When did you master talking like half my family?"

"Um, because I'm an actress."

He laughs. "Ah, of course."

After we've finished eating, we walk along the pier. The lights from the funfair behind us cast sparks of flashing colour on the ocean. I don't think I've visited the pier at night before. The sound of children's laughter has been replaced by loud rock music, and bright golden sunshine has been replaced by garish lighting, but the smells are just the same – sea salt mixed with deep-fried fast food.

We walk to the end of the pier and sit down on a wooden bench under a cast-iron street lamp. The breeze whips my ponytail around my shoulders, and I pull my cardigan tightly around me. Nate notices the wind has picked up and wraps his arm around my shoulder. I look up into his eyes. His expression is apprehensive, as if he's half expecting me to pull away, but I don't. I scoot closer towards him and relax when I feel his warm, hard body against mine.

"I love it here." The hand that is draped around me caresses my arm, and I feel so safe and rested that I respond with an almighty yawn.

"Oh my god, I'm so sorry," I say, covering my mouth.

"You've had a long day. Do you want to go back home?"

"No." I say quickly. "I mean, I *have* had a long day, but I absolutely do not want to go back home. I have the weekend off, so I can sleep tomorrow."

"I like the way you think," he says, beaming me one of his jaw-droppingly gorgeous smiles.

"And I like the way your face changes when you look at me. You use your whole body when you smile. It isn't just your mouth and your eyes. Your hair ruffles, your skin glows, the muscles in your chest tighten. It's quite remarkable. You have a big ol' sunshine grin."

Nate laughs and I tuck my head into the crook of his neck. I snake one of my arms around his middle and he responds by squeezing me tighter.

"You know, I think that's probably the nicest thing anyone has ever said to me."

He's still running his fingers down my arm, and the sensation, together with our closeness, is making my body heat up. My nipples tingle, sending a wild current of electricity between my legs. "Then I'm glad I said it."

I expect him to continue the conversation, but an odd silence fills the space between us. Nate's body stiffens. I lift up my head and gaze into his dark-brown eyes. "What is it?" I ask softly.

The angry vein from yesterday makes another appearance on the side of his head. "I didn't know anything about my father's connection to Aaron's supplier, and I feel terrible about it. Richie introduced me to Aaron and he trusted me. I let him down."

"It wasn't your fault."

He shakes his head. "I should have known. I'm supposed to be the MD of Klein & Co. I head up our UK operations, but it's clear my dad doesn't trust me with his business plans."

"He didn't trust you because he knows you'd put your friends first."

"And with him, business comes first." He lifts up his legs and rests his feet on the metal railings in front of us. "I told him."

I'm confused. "You told him what?"

"About my plans for the future. We got into an earth-shattering row after you left yesterday, and I told him. I can't do it any more, Freja. I don't want to be like him. Some days I don't even want to be a Klein. You said to me that you always want to feel like you're alive, but I feel like I can't breathe sometimes. I'm almost thirty and I'm the MD of one of Britain's largest tech companies, but I'd give it all up tomorrow to wait tables at your diner. Hell, I'd even wear the dress if it meant I could just . . . not be trapped anymore. I have a brother, a half-brother and two nephews. There are plenty more Kleins. It doesn't have to be me."

"Your father is proud of you. And he believes in you.

"And the whole world expects me to be grateful for that, but I didn't ask him if I could lead his empire, and I don't want to carry his legacy on my shoulders." He closes his eyes and shakes his head. "I sound like a spoiled rich kid, don't I? God, I hate that I sound like this, and I hate that everyone expects me to be just like him."

"Were you always closer to your mother?"

His body shifts awkwardly. He had the exact same reaction the last time his mother came up in conversation. "I guess so."

I don't want to ask the question, but it's begging. "How did she pass away?"

He lets out a long breath. "In a car accident when I was twelve. I lost my future that day, as well as my past. I was angry for so long. I needed her and she was gone. It's hard to explain what it feels like, to lose someone you loved that much . . . but it was a long time ago."

My eyes sting with tears as I piece together all the parts of who this man is. His name has forced him into a hard world – one where power and wealth is all that matters. He can't control the fact that he's part of a powerful family, but he can control whether or not he becomes an asshole like his father.

"My mother left me when I was eleven. I know what it's like to lose someone special to you at such a young age. I was always my father's daughter, but I still felt the loss. I needed therapy to get past my abandonment issues."

"Kleins don't do therapy," he says, his voice thick with regret. "We do stiff upper lips and then we silently move on. After my mother's funeral, my father refused to mention her name again, so neither did I. And I didn't talk about her with Sam either. Both of us were hurting and we couldn't share our feelings with each other. It was . . . just so fucking unhealthy. She was seeing another man when she died, you see. Dad had made her so unhappy that she sought comfort elsewhere. That's not something I judge her for – it's something I judge *him* for."

"It seems our lives have some parallels."

He pulls me closer and rests his head against mine. "I hope, as we get to know each other, we find more parallels. But with any luck, they won't be as tragic."

I hug him closer, thread my arm through his and take his hand. His skin is warm and his fingers feel like velvet. The rhythmic pounding between my thighs grows stronger as I give in to the urge, lift my hand to his face and kiss him.

The second my lips land on his, he leans in and

kisses me back. His mouth tastes like ketchup mixed with Pepsi Cola, which I never could have imagined would be this intoxicatingly sexy, but it is. His hand moves through my hair and his body melts against mine as our mouths, lips, tongues and teeth clash together in a wild and breathless tangle.

I move my hands to his chest, cursing the thick hooded sweatshirt I find under my fingertips. I want to feel his skin, so I touch his neck, caress his face, then I grab fistfuls of his hair and plunge my tongue deeper into his mouth.

He responds with a growl, but then he breaks away. His eyes gaze into mine with such intensity that the separation is agonising. "Will you come back to my hotel?"

"Try and stop me."

8

THE FIFTEEN-MINUTE CAR RIDE from Santa Monica to the Beverly Wilshire is torturous. Nate's chauffeur drives like he's the love child of Road Runner and Mr Magoo. He swings around a hairpin bend in the road, skimming inches from an articulated truck, and I half expect him to say "Meep meep". The fear of having my life cut short thanks to a chauffeur with cartoon driving skills is weirdly nowhere near as terrifying as the sexual tension building inside my body. I remind myself that Nate is champagne. I remind myself that he's bound to make me sick, but then carnal lust kicks in and my mind throws up images of very rude things I want to do to him. I worry about the content of my mind sometimes.

We're both belted into our seats and there are a good few inches separating us, which only strengthens my need to touch him, hold him, kiss him. His hand reaches for mine, and his fingers circle my wrist, then caress my palm. Long, delicious strokes trace a pattern from my pulse point to the centre of my forearm. I imagine him making the same movements on every inch of my body. I shiver as his breathing becomes louder, his fingers dancing with mine, then interlocking and releasing, only to repeat again as the agonising journey continues.

I'm disorientated when the car finally pulls up outside the hotel. Nate tells the chauffeur he'll call when he needs him again – sometime tomorrow –

and then a doorman opens the car door for me and I step outside. As the cool night air hits my flushed face I feel light-headed. All I can hear is my pulse pounding in my ears – I don't know if that's because my body is exhausted or super horny. If I googled the symptoms, there'd probably be overlap.

"You okay?" asks Nate. He takes hold of my hand and I fight the urge to leap into his arms and start making out. *Come on, Freja, just a couple more minutes. You can do it!*

"I'm good," I say as he leads me through the hotel doors – the same doors I barged my way through yesterday when I was dressed in my waitress uniform. Today, I look like I took a bath in my clothes and then let them dry on me. My leggings are sagging around the knee, and my oversized black t-shirt has faded to a dirty grey following too many washes.

We make a beeline for the elevators. Bright yellow artificial light streams from the ceilings and creates a dazzling display on the floor in front of me. It's almost midnight, but throngs of guests are still in the lobby, some heading for their rooms, while others mill around the bar and restaurant. I felt conspicuous when I came here yesterday in my diner uniform, but tonight I notice there's a mix of people. One girl we pass has on the most gorgeous fuchsia-pink evening dress I've ever seen. She sashays in the direction of the bar and wraps her arm around a guy in a dashing tux. We pass a group of tourists wearing baseball caps, Disneyland shirts and carrying bags full of vacation souvenirs.

"I'm on the top floor," Nate says as we wait for an elevator to arrive. I stuff my cardigan into my tote and hope nobody else wants to ride with us, because all the rude things I imagined doing in the car have retaken residence in my brain, and I don't trust myself not to jump his bones the second we're alone.

I hear a pinging sound. We spin around and walk into the elevator behind us. We're alone, but just as the doors start to close, the Disneyland tourists descend and one of them slams his chubby hand between the doors.

I step forward and fix him with a glare. "This elevator is full."

The white-haired guy just stares at me. His mouth falls open and his eyes expand to almost the same size as the ears on his silly Mickey Mouse cap. I feel sorry for him because I sound mean. I also feel sorry for him because he appears to have sunburnt his spongy nose.

I press the button for the top floor and the doors close again.

Nate opens his mouth to speak, but his words get lost on my tongue as I plunge for his lips. He flips me around so my back is against the elevator wall and pushes my arms above my head. His hands hold me firmly in place while he plants ravenous kisses on my neck, then my chest, and then along my jawline.

Nate's hands move down my body, then he grabs my ass and lifts me off the floor. I coil my legs around his waist and he pushes me up against the elevator wall with so much force that the air gets knocked from my lungs. I could fuck him right now, but the second the idea of kinky elevator-sex sends a rush of desire cascading between my thighs, the golden doors ping, then swish open.

Nate doesn't put me down.

His strong arms hold onto me as he briefly substitutes the elevator wall with the marbled hotel wall, planting kisses on every inch of exposed skin, before carrying me down the corridor.

We arrive outside a dark oak door labelled "Veranda Suite" just as Nate's kisses become more fervent. "I am so fucking turned on right now," he whispers breathlessly into my ear as he reaches into his pocket, fumbles around and then drops his wallet. "Damn it."

We both start to laugh. He eases me to my feet, picks up his wallet and finds his room key. I drape my arms around him and nuzzle against the soft olive skin of his neck.

"Wait," he says, placing the key in the lock.

I drop my arms. "What is it?"

"I don't want you to think I do this all the time."

"Do what all the time? Bring women as fabulous as me back to your hotel room?"

He cocks his head to one side and gives me his sunshine grin. "Something like that."

"I wouldn't care if you did, but it's impossible anyway. I'm one in a million."

"You can say that again."

The second we're through the door, I drop my tote and my gaze lands on a gigantic four-poster bed. "My god," Nate says. "I want you so much."

He pulls the neck of my t-shirt down over my shoulder and sucks and bites at my skin. I moan as the sharp stings send my desire soaring. I rake my hand through his hair, my breathing becoming shallower. "Please, I need . . ."

106

His head snaps up. "I know," he says with a low growl. His hands snake under my t-shirt. "I know what you need, and I'm going to give it to you."

Holy fucking shit. His sex-words are as hot as his sex-actions. He pulls my top over my head and takes my shell-pink-satin-covered breasts in his hands. His head dips and his tongue sinks into my cleavage, then he pushes one of my bra straps down and scoops out my breast. He rolls my nipple between his fingers as he finds my mouth again. "Oh fuck," I moan against his tongue as he pinches hard.

"Tell me if I'm too rough," he says. Our mouths barely leave each other's bodies as we shed more clothing. His hooded jacket falls to the floor with a thump, followed by his t-shirt, then we both poke off our sneakers with our toes.

"Don't worry about that. I can be quite rough myself." I feel the full length of him, rock-hard and eager, under his denim jeans. I grapple with his belt and buttons until I have enough room to reach inside his pants and place my hands around him.

"Oh sweet Jesus," he groans as my grip tightens. I turn our bodies around and push him up against the wall. Then I fall to my knees, yank his pants and shorts down to his ankles and begin teasing his cock with my mouth.

One of his arms drops against the wall with a thud. I look up at him, and my excitement builds when I see the ecstasy on his face. I work my tongue over his tip, each movement eliciting shivery breaths and guttural moans from him as his ass bucks against the wall. I take him completely into my mouth, and his hands move to my head, grappling with my hair tie. When my hair falls free, he twists his fingers through it.

"Stop . . ." He's breathing in short, desperate puffs and I recognise the signal that he's getting close already. "Stop," he says again. "I want . . . If you don't slow down, this could be over in five seconds."

I swap my mouth for my hand, stroking him gently as I rise to my feet. "We could slow down, or we could finish up now and then do it all over again." I bring my bruised lips to his chest and trace circles on his warm skin with my tongue.

"You're fucking insatiable," he says, reaching behind my back to unclasp my bra.

"I prefer to use the word 'greedy'." I push my bra straps over my arms. His eyes go to my chest, and his mouth follows. He grazes the sensitive skin of one nipple with his teeth, then he pinches the other hard. My vagina reacts to the sharp pain with contractions that settle into a pulsating throb. "Oh fuck. I need you to fuck me now."

He walks me back and lowers me onto the four-poster bed. "Shit, I need to get a condom. Just a second."

He practically sprints through the open archway into the bathroom. I take the opportunity to remove my totally unsexy, baggy-knee leggings. Ugh. I must be packing some inner non-visual hotness if I can manage to pull a guy like Nate while looking like . . . Jesus Christ, my brain almost said "while looking like I wait tables for a living", but that's exactly what I do. Given I'm also in the Wilshire, the *Pretty Woman* parallels are off the scale. I tell myself I absolutely do *not* look like a prostitute.

Nate returns with an entire box of Durex in his hand. I figure he took my previous suggestion that we fuck fast then repeat it literally. He takes out a packet, opens the silver foil wrapper with his teeth and rolls the condom on.

I rise to my knees, letting my fingers run over the sweat-drenched muscles of his chest. One of his hands holds firm to my jawline as our mouths meet again; the other dips into my panties. "You're so wet," he says as his fingers explore. He stops kissing me for a moment, gazing hungrily into my eyes. "I want to watch you come."

More sex-words. I think if he just spoke filth to me all night without any touching or kissing or fucking, I'd be able to orgasm.

One strong hand steadies my hip while the other explores. I place both of my hands on his shoulders, and he pushes my panties down to the tops of my thighs. His fingers rub through my folds in a delicious rhythm, his thumb massaging my clit in sweeping movements that take my breath away. One of his fingers plunges deep inside me and he holds it there, pressing hard against my vaginal walls as his thumb moves faster.

A soft whimper escapes my throat as he caresses my most sensitive spot. "That's it," he says. His voice is thick with desire. "Let me see you come."

I look into his eyes. His pupils are enlarged, almost eclipsing his dark irises. I watch him watch me, and our gazes lock. He's holding me with a force so strong and powerful that I have to bite down hard on my bottom lip to stop myself screaming out his name. How is it possible to have this kind of connection with a virtual stranger? How do we fit together so perfectly?

Pressure builds in my groin as his fingers move more rapidly over me and inside me. I grip his neck hard when the twisting, rippling waves of pleasure soar from every part of me that he's touching. I let the intensity wash over me, moaning and shrieking as my body shakes. When the orgasm ends, I fall into his arms, my breath shallow and rasping. He smoothes my hair from my face and kisses me tenderly.

"That was awesome," he says, helping me to lie down on my back. He slides my panties off my legs and lowers his head to lay kisses on my stomach. He sinks his tongue into my navel, then plays join the dots with my freckles and his tongue. "You're so beautiful."

He begins to move on top of me, but I twist around in his arms and push him onto his back. My taking control knocks the wind out of him for a moment, but when I smile, toss my hair over my shoulder and straddle him, his expression changes. He lies back, relaxes against the fluffy white pillows and watches the show.

I grab hold of his cock and gently ease myself down onto him. His entire body braces in anticipation as I take in his full length. "Oh yes," he groans when he feels me around him. I build up a rhythm, moving up and down, bucking my hips gently. He grabs hold of my ass and thrusts upwards into me, both of us hot and sweaty and breathing as if each breath could be our last.

I fall forward as I ride him, my palms resting on his chest for balance, then our eyes find each other's again. He watches me like before, silently but with even more fire. One of his hands moves up to my neck while the other grips my ass. His body seems to work on instinct, meeting my body's movements with thrusts of his own until he's shrieking his own release into my hair.

I reach down to touch his face, caressing his strong jaw as he lies silently beneath me. I can't think of anything to say to him. I'm still trying to process what just happened to me – and not just my orgasm. The strength of the emotions I'm feeling has taken me by surprise. As I gaze into his beautiful dark-brown irises, my breathing turns into a weak sob. I feel my eyes water. Crap! I don't want this. I don't want to fall this hard.

I lie down on my back next to him. He turns on his side, but the expression on his face has changed. The ghostlike remains of his sunshine smile mixed with yearning have been replaced with a look of complete confusion. A ridge appears between his brows. "Are you okay?" he asks with concern in his voice.

Damn it. Why do I have to be such an idiot? "I'm more than okay," I say, pushing everything else out of my mind. I start to kiss him again, but he stops me.

"Hey," he says, holding both my hands tightly in his. "What is it?"

"Nothing." I force my eyes dry. "Just silliness."

"Freja," he says, drawing out my name.

I exhale a shaky breath and curse myself for being so pathetic. "I just feel a bit overwhelmed. You don't really know this about me yet, but . . . well, I guess I feel things a little too deeply sometimes."

He leans close and reaches out to touch my hair. "I want to get to know everything about you – and I will."

A quiet laugh escapes my lips. "You seem very sure of that."

"I am sure." He kisses the top of my head. "I'd live the rest of my life a very happy man if I was spending every day getting to know you."

His hands wrap around my body. I take hold of his jaw, my gaze sweeping over his ruffled hair and soft lips. "You don't know what you're letting yourself in for."

He cocks his head and delivers a killer smirk. "I'll take a punt, as long as there's a money-back guarantee." I playfully bat his chest and he responds with a delicious laugh.

I snuggle against him, enjoying how his naked body feels against mine. "What happens when you go home?" The second the words leap off my tongue, I want to catch them and swallow them back down. I cringe at how needy I must sound to him.

"*If* I go home."

My heart leaps. "Do you mean . . . ?"

He nods. "The business idea I have could be started anywhere – in any city."

"But all your family is in England."

"And all my friends are here."

Is he including me in that? I close my eyes and wrap my arms around him. He untangles one of the bed sheets and drapes it over us.

The last thing I remember is his breath blowing softly against my cheek.

9

I WAKE UP TO BRIGHT sunshine and quiet jazz music. I'm alone in a cool bed, half my body encased in crisp white sheets. I stretch out as my vision adjusts to the daylight, and I see Nate sitting at a polished walnut table which is stacked high with important-looking files and business papers. He smiles when he notices me stirring, and I smile back.

"Morning, sleepyhead," he says affectionately. He takes off his glasses – woah! Since when did he wear glasses? – then walks over and sits down next to me on the bed. "It's almost eleven, but I didn't want to wake you." He reaches out and smoothes my hair from my face. "I figured you needed it."

"It's that late?" I say, shocked I've managed to sleep for so long. "I guess it was an eventful night."

"The best," he says with a beaming smile. "Even better than I imagined."

I sit up and wrap the sheet around me. "So, just how long have you spent imagining us doing that?"

"Pretty much every night since I met you."

I laugh. "Oh my god, you're just going to be that honest about it?"

"I'm a man, Freja." He throws me a devilish smirk. "*And* the first time I met you, you kinda left a big impression."

"Ah, right," I say, laughing at the week-old memory. "Mickey and Minnie."

"Uh-huh." He leans in close and caresses my breasts through the bed sheet as he kisses me. "*They're* better than I imagined too."

I deepen our kiss and glide my hands through his damp hair. He must have showered already. I inhale the fresh, cool smell of his body, and all the feelings from last night return in a blast of sexiness that makes me groan from my toes.

"I think I might be ready for round two," he says, fire in his eyes.

"I think I might need to pee."

He laughs as he kisses me. "I can wait."

I drop the sheet, but hesitate before getting up. "I don't suppose you have a spare toothbrush?" I figure I can use his shampoo and shower gel, but sharing toothbrushes is a step too far. Which is ridiculous considering how much time I spent exploring his mouth last night.

He gets off the bed and picks up three shiny gift bags. "You're in luck. I sent Sandy, my dad's PA, on a spree with my credit card earlier."

I remember the timid girl with the huge dark eyes from the business meeting I barged into. Is shopping for her boss's son's overnight visitor part of her job description? I apprehensively look into the bags. "*Min Gud*!"

"Min what now?"

"What on earth has she bought? Are these for me to . . . keep?" I curse myself as soon as the words leave my mouth, but the designer-labelled gifts look seriously expensive. I have another scary *Pretty Woman*-parallel moment. "Nate, this is too much. I can't accept this."

He looks puzzled for a moment, but then his

114

expression softens with realisation. "I understand, but it's fine. I hoped you'd stay for the rest of the day, and I didn't want to have to work around going back to the house for the things you'd need, so I got you these. I couldn't send Sandy all the way to Target when Rodeo Drive is a thirty-second walk from here. It didn't occur to me you'd feel uncomfortable, but I guess it should have."

I look into the bags: Dolce & Gabbana dress, Bally shoes, La Perla lingerie and a bag with expensive toiletries inside. There's even a hairbrush. "This is really thoughtful, but . . ."

"I'm sorry, I didn't think," he says in a regretful tone.

"No, I'm being silly. And super ungrateful. It's a lovely gesture."

I pull out an absolutely gorgeous white sundress with a fitted bodice from the Dolce & Gabbana bag. The dress has a Mediterranean pattern featuring bright yellow lemons, orange flowers and royal-blue paintbrush swirls. I don't usually wear this much colour – and I avoid orange for obvious hair-related reasons – but it's incredibly beautiful.

"It's gorgeous, isn't it?"

"Yes, but how did she know my size . . . and oh, sweet Jesus!" My jaw drops to the floor when I spot the price tag. "Nate, this dress cost a thousand dollars."

"Okay . . . I guess I should have removed the tag."

I'm too busy hyperventilating to speak.

"And I checked your clothes for your size. But not in a creepy way. I mean, your shoes are just there, and your t-shirt . . . I swear this was just me being spontaneous this morning. You said you weren't busy today, so I thought we could do something, and one thought led to another thought, which lead to me calling Sandy, and here we are. I've ordered a late breakfast with room service too – I just need to call them and they'll bring it all up. But if you want, or if you *do* have plans, I can drop you back home. Whatever you want to do is fine."

My stomach growls at the thought of food. All I ate yesterday was a handful of pine nuts and a hot dog. I'd love to spend the day with Nate, but there's something about getting swept off my feet by a dashing blue-blooded Englishman that seems totally off-the-scale unreal and gives me a weird, unsettling feeling. I want to see where this goes. I want to be confident and unafraid, but I'm not either of those things with him. "Thank you for all of this," I say, pushing the dress to one side. I lie back down on the bed. "I need to use the bathroom, but we'll talk after breakfast."

He cocks an eyebrow and his beautiful dark eyes crease at the corners. "That sounds ominous."

I reach up to touch his face. He's had a shave this morning. His skin is as smooth as silk. "I promise it won't be ominous. Unless you've got some big terrible secret you're hiding from me."

"Ah, busted," he says with a wicked smirk. "I have a crazy ex-wife chained up in my attic back home."

"Funny." I get out of bed, pick up the bag of toiletries and cross the short distance to the bathroom. I feel Nate's eyes watching me. "Are you staring at my ass?"

"If I said no would you accuse me of lying?" he

calls.

I turn on the shower. "Yes."

* * *

I make good use of the ultra-expensive, but totally luxurious, shampoo and shower gel gift set that Sandy bought for me. After blow-drying my hair, I emerge from the bathroom, where I'm greeted by a trolley stocked with fresh fruit and pastries. My stomach growls its approval.

"I thought we could have a champagne breakfast," says Nate, popping the cork on a bottle of Bollinger. I ask myself if I'd want to swap the champagne for a steaming cup of hot chocolate, and for the first time in my life, my brain screams "Are you fucking crazy?" back at me.

I readjust my towel, sit down at the table and dive in, picking a freshly baked croissant out of a basket lined with checked paper. "I should probably get dressed," I say, eyeing Nate's dark lounge pants and t-shirt. He looks fabulous in black.

"You're fine just as you are." He pours the champagne and sits down opposite me. "And your hair looks amazing. I love your hair. It totally embodies who you are: distinctive, bold and fiery."

"I wish you could seek out my old school friends and tell them that. It was tough being the only ginger in a school filled with blonde children. They used to call me Carrot Head." I take a sip of my drink, the bubbles fizzing against my tongue. "This is really lovely."

"I'm glad you approve. I haven't had breakfast

117

here since I arrived. Between you and me, I'm a bit of a Denny's man."

"No way."

He nods. "Can't beat American bacon. Or pancakes." He picks up a bread roll and slices it open. "So, what would be on my breakfast table back in Copenhagen?"

"*Wienerbrød*," I say with a giggle. I pick a flaky pastry filled with gooey custard out of the basket and place it on his plate. "You'd call it a Danish."

He laughs and takes a sip of champagne. "After meeting you, I'll never look at a Danish pastry in the same way again."

I give him an amused look. "Are you calling me flaky?"

"No, I'm saying I'll never forget you."

My belly goes all fluttery and I feel my cheeks flush. I bring my champagne glass to my lips, but that weird crazy feeling returns, twisting my stomach into a loop. I put the glass back down on the table and nervously clear my throat.

"Is this when we talk about the things that aren't ominous?"

I sigh heavily. I'm frustrated with myself. I'm a great believer in sharing. If worries aren't shared, they're internalised, then magnified, and all of a sudden a problem that could have been easily solved has become a chaotic mess of epic, unfixable proportions, glued together with anxiety and bundled up with fear. "Did you know I was married once?"

He stops chewing his bread roll and swallows hard. A big lump of food bulges in his neck. Christ, I hope he doesn't choke. "No, Richie didn't tell me that. You must have been very young."

"It was six years ago. I was nineteen."

"Nineteen? Crikey. I was an immature man-baby when I was nineteen."

"Well, I wasn't particularly mature either. I have no regrets, but it wasn't the smartest decision I ever made. Per and I had known each other since high school. We left for university together in Sweden, then one weekend in December I decided it would be fun to get married in Lapland at Midwinter under the Northern Lights. Sometimes I do that. I get a wild and crazy idea in my head and I have to see it through. That's how I'm here – one day I decided I'd become an actress, the next day I bought a plane ticket to LA."

His eyes twinkle with a trace of a smile. "But the wild and crazy marriage didn't work out?"

"No, we divorced after eighteen months. I guess I must have been high on the solstice, or the Northern Lights, or elf magic. Per is a good man – a really good man – but I guess, after time, he just couldn't keep up with what I wanted."

"Because you want to live." He echoes my answer to the question he asked me on our first date. *What do you want, Freja Larsen?*

"Living my life this way is like purposely sailing a ship into a storm just to see if you can survive. I shouldn't have married Per. I knew we weren't right for each other, but I thought I could make him right for me. Our marriage failed because I was sailing a completely different ship to him. It would have had the same outcome whether we were enjoying the calm or riding the storm together."

Nate rests his back against the soft, cushioned

chair. "You said you knew Per wasn't right for you. Did you expect him to change?"

"No, I wanted to change myself." A rush of painful memories surfaces. Blame, rage, hate, therapy . . . determination to not be like her. "This is the ominous part," I say with a touch of humour. "I never got on with my mother. My dad said we were too much alike – both headstrong, both ambitious, both always searching for something more than we had. When she left us, it was a bad time. I grew to despise everything about her, including the characteristics we shared. It took me years to learn to love myself again, and Per was a good friend through all of that. He's a scriptwriter for TV now, but when we were students we talked about writing plays and putting on great productions together. I imagined owning a nice apartment in Copenhagen, maybe a couple of dogs, perhaps we'd even have a little garden. I could act in plays, and teach, and a few years down the line we'd have a couple of kids – just normal stuff most girls my age expected they'd have one day. I married Per to convince myself I could be normal. I did love him, but I also used him. If I married my best friend and learned to be content, I could prove to the world that I wasn't like my mother."

"Do you think you *are* like her?"

"Yes, in many ways." I take a kiwi fruit from the bowl and cut into it. "But it took me a while to realise that it's our choices in life that make us who we are, not our personality traits. I may have inherited her restlessness, her ambition and her zest for life, but I don't have to make the same choices she did."

Nate takes a small bunch of grapes from the fruit bowl. "I envy you."

"You do?"

He pops a grape in his mouth. "Yeah, it's like you're in love with being alive and you have no regrets." His expression shifts for a moment. His beautiful dark eyelashes cast a melancholy shadow on his cheek as he lowers his gaze. "I wish I could find the same kind of peace." A smile dimples his face, but it doesn't reach his eyes.

"Your dad?"

"It's really difficult," he says. "Dad's given me so much, but at the same time he hasn't given me anywhere near enough." He flicks the crumbs on his plate, reflecting how lost he is in his thoughts. "I don't really talk about this stuff, but you're so easy to talk to."

"You told me that before." I reach forward and place my hand over his. He looks up and threads his fingers through mine. "How did you leave things with him?"

"He threatened to destroy my career and I told him to go fuck himself."

"Oh," I say, giving his hand a squeeze. "Not great then."

"No, but we've said worse to each other, several times. Dad demands respect, gratitude and unconditional support from the people who serve him, and he includes his children in that."

Jeez, his dad is definitely somewhere between asshole and bastard on the bad-guy scale. For once I'm lost for words. "I'm sorry. I'm usually a giver of great advice, but this has me stumped."

"You've helped me so much already." He

121

caresses my hand with his fingertips, his gaze fixed on the physical connection he's making. "You stormed into that meeting, fought for your friend, and you didn't give a shit about who my father was. I've never seen that before."

Holy crap, he's talking as if his father *is* Don Corleone. Am I going to wake up with a horse's head in my bed tomorrow? "It's not that I didn't give a shit who he was, it's that I didn't really *know* who he was. And like I said, I have spontaneity issues."

He shakes his head. "This isn't about you being spontaneous. It's about you not being afraid to stand up to him. My heart was in my mouth, but it was still the sexiest thing I've ever seen. That's why I envy you. You're living by your own rules, but I'm living by someone else's – my father's. I was born to inherit Klein & Co, so everyone back home will think my leaving is terrible. And yet staying is unthinkable."

"I understand." He loosens his grip on my hand and I lightly stroke his forearm. "You can't live your life if you're letting someone else direct it. Even if that someone is your father."

"I know, and now he knows." My hand is still holding his arm when he stands up and moves around the table. I stand up too. His hands move to my waist, and mine go to his shoulders. "What do you say we make good use of those strawberries?"

My eyes flit to the white bowl filled with fragrant red fruit. "Whatever do you mean, Mr Klein?" I ask with fake innocence.

He picks a small strawberry out of the bowl and rubs it against my bottom lip. "Bite." I let him place the fruit between my teeth. Then he brings his mouth to mine and we eat together, our tongues sliding into each other's mouths, finishing up in a kiss that tastes like it's been blessed by the gods of summertime – sticky, sweet and sexy.

He pulls the towel from my body, picks up another strawberry and trails it down my chest. "I guess I'm showering again," I say with a moan as he teases one of my nipples with his tongue.

He squeezes the fruit and spreads the pink juice all over my breasts. "You mightn't need to. I intend to clean it all off like this."

He leans down and proceeds to run his tongue over one of my boobs while gently kneading the other. He pulls at my nipple until it's hard and pebbled. I inhale sharply when his licks and sucks grow stronger, his tongue moving over my breasts, lapping gently until I smell like I should be baked in a shortcake.

"Come with me." He picks up the bowl of strawberries and takes my hand, leading me to the unmade bed. "You took control last night, but now it's my turn."

"Control?" I ask mischievously. "I thought we were both big on personal freedom?" I sit down on the bed.

"To quote that film you like, 'I'll think about that tomorrow . . .' or when I'm finished doing this."

I laugh as he lowers me down on the bed. He pulls his t-shirt over his head, and I can see his pants are already tenting around his groin – a sight which makes a rush of heat spread wildly between my legs.

He takes the largest of the strawberries and

places it on my navel. I smirk when I see the look on his face: it's a strange mix of lustiness and naughtiness. He picks more strawberries out of the bowl, placing them strategically around my body – my nipples, the valley between my breasts, my throat, my pelvis – all of his favourite kissing spots. His fingers trail my thighs, and my pulse races when I realise what he's planning. He puts a strawberry at the top of each thigh, then he gently separates my folds and places the final fruit at my entrance.

He stands back and admires his work. "You know, I reckon it wouldn't be too much of a stretch to win the Turner Prize for this. All I'd have to do was think of some ridiculously highbrow artistic meaning for why I'd placed strawberries on your best bits and I'd have the trophy in the bag."

"Would I have to lie on a plinth in an art gallery?"

He starts to sweat. "Yes, and fuck me, wouldn't that be hot?" I laugh and a strawberry rolls off my boob. "You'd have to keep statue-still, though."

"It is kinda hard to balance it on there, you know. It's not a sea lion's nose."

Nate twists his face up and I giggle. Both strawberries fall off my boobs, and the one on my throat rolls away and lands near my earlobe. "See, what you did now, jiggle-jugs? You've turned my beautiful art display into a circus." He pops one of the strawberries into my mouth and kisses me again, then he starts eating his way down my body.

Attempting to stay completely motionless is practically impossible when a super-hot guy with the bronzed, muscular torso of a Roman gladiator is licking strawberry juice off your tits. I inhale the delicious fragrance and my toes curl. When he's finished with my upper body, he pops another strawberry into my mouth and kisses me as I eat it. Our tongues taste divine, the flavour still ripe in his mouth long after I've swallowed.

Nate picks up the fruit from my stomach and squeezes it, making a pool of pink liquid in my navel. He eats the fruit's flesh from his fingers, then he laps the juice off my stomach. The flicks of his tongue strike in a rhythm which synchronises with the rapid beat of my heart. His mouth travels to my pelvis, then my thighs. He shares the fruit with me, until all that's left is the large strawberry he placed between my legs.

The second I see Nate's head dip down the muscles of my vagina begin to throb sharply. "*Åh min Gud*," I moan, my voice suddenly hoarse.

He pushes my legs slightly apart, then pokes the strawberry around my opening with his teeth. For a second I worry that he might try to insert it further into me, but he removes it and squeezes a small amount of juice onto his hand instead.

"What are you doing?" I ask.

He answers me with a smile and a kiss as he reaches down and spreads the juice inside me.

"Are you going to eat me now?" My voice is throaty and effortlessly alluring.

He rubs what's left of the fruit over my clit, sending waves of intensity rippling throughout my lower body. "That was always my plan," he says. His mouth dives between my legs, and I have to catch my breath. His tongue tastes every inch of me while his hands hold tight to my hips. I arch my

125

back when he sucks juice and strawberry flesh from my clit, his tongue circling and flicking as he grunts hungrily.

It only takes a few seconds for my orgasm to take control of my body. I shake fiercely against his mouth, throwing my head back against the thick pillows and twisting in the tangled sheets until the electric current subsides. But he continues his feast, licking and sucking on my body until I feel the tension start to build again.

Foodie sex should be remembered with its very own day of awareness, because there must be so many people on the planet who have no idea how good it is. I shriek loudly as I let myself go for a second time. The carnal screams rise from deep within my body, shaking torrents of pleasure on ragged breaths. "That . . . was . . . fucking . . . amazing," I say between pants.

He crawls up my body, his cock digging into my side. He lays his head next to mine. He's so close that his nose nuzzles against my cheek. "You taste amazing," he says with a purr to his tone.

"If that's how you like to eat, then you may dine any time you want." I stroke his clammy cheek. "Do you want me to sort you out down there?"

I feel the length of him under his clothes and he groans. "How about you formulate a plan of action while I assist you in the shower?"

"Make it a bubble bath, and you're on."

10

WE SPEND A ROMANTIC AFTERNOON at Venice Beach, then have an early dinner at the High Rooftop Lounge. It's a Saturday, so naturally my cell phone has buzzed itself into oblivion all day long with friends wondering where I am and, more importantly, where I'll be tonight. Dana and Marie want me to join them at Boulevard3 because they've heard Nickelback are in town. I don't ask how Dana knows they'll be at that specific nightclub because the answer is always the same – "I have my contacts." JJ, meanwhile, asks me flat out if I've "screwed the hot English guy yet". I ignore him and get devilish satisfaction from knowing how desperate he is to hear all the juicy details. I have two messages from Logan, the kindergarten teacher, who *still* can't accept we're over – despite me sending five previous texts and one verbal conversation where I said the exact words "We're over". The guy has a screw loose. I'm wondering if flying a helicopter over his house with a banner saying "We're over" on it is my last option when I receive a baffling message from Peyton: *I'm worried about Richie. Have you spoken to him? Do you know where he is?* I show the message to Nate.

"Oh, shit, I feel bad," he says, throwing down enough dollars to pay for our food and drink bill twice over. "I fly over here, drop a huge bombshell on him, and then leave him to it. I need to spend some time with him. I said I'd have drinks with my dad tonight, but I'll call my car, drop you back home and see how the ground lies with him first."

We leave the bar and take a taxi back to the hotel. I text Peyton to let her know I'll be home in an hour. She replies that she hasn't seen Richie since yesterday and she's had to rope in her mother to watch Riley so she can work a late shift at the diner. Anxiety knots in my stomach. This isn't like Richie. I curse myself for having the best night of my life while all this was happening. I can tell from the look on Nate's face and the way he keeps checking the time on his cell phone every thirty seconds that he's worried too.

When we get back to the Beverly Wilshire, Nate takes my arm and leads me through the glass doors. What a difference a thousand-dollar dress makes. The snooty hotel guests are no longer looking at me as if I eat garbage out of trashcans.

"My phone is almost out of charge. I need to get my spare and swap the sim card over," Nate says.

"I'll wait here for the car."

He gives me a peck on the cheek. "I'll be five minutes."

I walk over to a small seating area in front of a tall mirror and take out my cell phone again. There's no further update from Peyton, but Todd Warner has sent an odd message complaining that Reed doesn't want him to wear a modesty "cock sock" during Monday's shoot. I shudder at the thought of how long it's going to take him to psych himself up for our next sex scene given it took all freaking day for him to find the courage to touch my boob.

The chair next to me screeches along the polished floor as the figure of a man in an expensive suit sits down. I'm immediately hit by Lord Klein's aura of evil. He crosses his legs, straightens his tie and adjusts his cufflinks. My stomach sinks. I smile politely, but he doesn't smile back. His face is lined with harsh angles and creases.

"Shouldn't you be serving hamburgers and French fries today?" Lord Klein's steely grey eyes stare into mine. His demeanour is unpleasant – in a gut-wrenching, flesh-crawling kinda way.

"No," I reply. "Clearly, I'm not waitressing today." I turn back to my phone. My heart rate picks up speed. *Don't let him get to you. Don't let him win.*

"Ah, it's hard to keep up." His deep voice is patronising and scoffing. "Maybe I should have asked if you'd be performing sexual acts in front of a camera today."

Bile rises into my throat, my gut burning with rage. How does he know? "No, clearly, I'm not acting today either."

Lord Klein leans forward in his seat. "Look at me, girl," he barks. His clipped English accent is strained with aggression. I will Nate to hurry up, but I refuse to turn my head. "Fine, you can listen. I've had my people look into you. Does my son know you take your clothes off in cheap soft-porn movies? Does he know he's fucking you after half of Hollywood has already been there?"

My heart starts to thud through my ribcage. Would Nate forgive me if I punched his father to the ground? He probably would, but I might get arrested, so I summon some strength instead. "You're trying very hard to hurt me, but it won't work," I say, quietly but confidently. I meet his gaze and hold it, managing to block out the fear that is coursing through my veins.

Lord Klein laughs. "No, girl, I'm only here to tell you how we're going to proceed from this point forward. I know you stayed at this hotel last night, and I also know you're just one bounced paycheck away from pornography. Take this as a warning – Nathaniel will not be your meal ticket."

I let his words wash over me and I plaster a fake smile onto my face. "You don't know anything about me."

"I know you were born in Copenhagen and you're twenty-five years old. Your father, Hans, is a retired vet. He has a criminal record for farming cannabis, and for disrupting the peace at a climate change protest. You have one sister, Sara, who is a police officer, and an ex-husband, Per, who writes for Danish television. Your mother, Silje, currently lives between homes in France, Spain and Italy, with her second husband. You've seen her only a handful of times in the last fourteen years. You spent three years in therapy then you studied theatre at the University of Uppsala in Sweden. You had a few acting jobs in Denmark before you moved here. You currently work part-time at the Cosmic Diner on Route 66 and you're about to finish your second year at UCLA. You started working on a film for Twilight Studios last week, but the film is having financial difficulties – just like your roommates. And just like you."

His voice is full of triumph as he reels off the

information. I wonder if the person – or people – who dug into my background wondered why on earth they were being asked to do it. "I'm not ashamed of my life, Lord Klein," I force my tone to remain upbeat. "There's also nothing I haven't already shared with Nate."

His jaw stiffens and his eyes flame. "I don't expect shame. I expect you to know your place. See that beautiful woman over there?"

"My place?" I say, slightly amused by Klein's overly dramatic putdowns. I follow his gaze to the blonde woman who arrived at Aaron's meeting with Nate. She's talking with Nate's brother, Sam, dressed in a burgundy tailored dress which matches her plump lips. She glances at us briefly, her golden hair falling over her shoulders in thick, glossy waves.

"That's Evelyn Ashby-Ledger. I consider her part of my family. She's my business partner's only daughter, and she has more grace, class and elegance in her little finger than you have in your entire body." The comment is so theatrically ridiculous that I want to giggle. His petty insults belong on the stage. Even if Evelyn *is* more elegant, classy and graceful than I am, who gives a fuck? I'm certainly not in a hurry to sign my inadequate ass up for charm school. "Evelyn writes a fashion column for a British magazine, and I'm investing in her new fashion label. *She* is an appropriate partner for my son."

Jesus Christ, it's like I've stepped into a fairy tale and I'm one poisoned apple away from a glass coffin. "I'm sure Evelyn is lovely, and I've no reason to doubt she's all of the things you say she

131

is, but I've only known your son for a week. We live on two different continents. Nevertheless, I think he might be old enough to decide who he wants to spend his time with."

Lord Klein spots Nate walking into the lobby from the elevators and sits up straight. "I'll keep this simple for you. If Evelyn is Chanel, then you're Walmart. Men like my son do not plan futures with girls like you."

"What the hell is going on?" Nate asks, his eyes firing shots of mistrust at his father.

The older man stands up, re-buttons his suit jacket and fixes his firm gaze upon his son. "Just reintroducing myself to Miss Larsen, Nathaniel," he says. Nate's gaze shifts between us, his brow pleated with intense suspicion. How is it possible that he is the son of that bastard? "We're having dinner at seven thirty, so I expect to see you back here for drinks no later than nine."

Nate's jaw braces and the angry vein returns to the side of his face. "I'll be back when I'm done. *If* I'm done."

"If you want my advice, I think *she's* been done enough already," says the lord.

Nate is on him immediately. "What the hell did you just say?" he roars. With his height, build and relative youth, he towers over his father.

Evelyn and Sam rush forward. Sam, who is shorter and stockier than Nate, takes hold of his brother's arm. "Not here," he says.

Nate yanks his arm out of Sam's grip and squares off against the older man. "Freja, could you step outside please? I have something I want to say to my father."

I don't budge. He looks like he's close to knocking his father's yellowed teeth out of his head. "I really need to get back home," I say, hoping he'll drop it. "Now."

He takes a step back. "I'm coming with you."

Klein replaces his smarmy look with an irritating grin that makes my skin crawl. "Just make sure you're here for dinner." He walks away and Evelyn follows him. Sam gives his brother a reassuring pat on the shoulder before joining them.

When we're alone, my mind starts to race. Insecurity, unworthiness and shame creep around under my skin, giving me goosebumps. A swirl of nausea settles into the pit of my stomach. I do my best to push the unfamiliar feelings away. I protectively wrap my arms around my body, trying to hold it together.

"What did he say to you?" Nate gently touches my arm, his eyes sweeping over mine.

I'm about to excuse his father. The words appear carelessly on the tip of my tongue – "Nothing", "It doesn't matter", "Just forget about it" – all those things women learn we should say, the natural consequence of being made to feel less than you are.

"Freja, we aren't going anywhere until you tell me what my father said to you."

"Do you want it in depth or the highlight reel?"

"The highlights will do. If I'm not coming back here tonight, I'd rather know quickly so I can look forward to another night with you."

I nip at my bottom lip. *Jeez, hold it together, Freja. Holde det sammen.* "He's had someone dig into my past. He knows all about my family, my

133

career and my years in therapy. Not that I have any terrible dark secrets – you already know everything."

"What?" Nate's face is distorted with disgust and disbelief. "I swear to god, Freja, I could go down there right now and knock seven bells out of that man. I am so sorry he did this."

I hesitate for a moment about telling him the rest. "He told me men like you don't get with girls like me – they end up with women like Evelyn. He compared me to Walmart and her to Chanel."

His mouth falls open, then he swallows hard. "Freja . . . I swear, I will make him pay for this. And Evelyn is just a friend, I told you already she—"

"I know, I know." I feel water pool in my eyes and I scrunch up my nose to stop the tears rolling down my face. I'm not letting that awful man have my tears – I'm not. "We've only known each other a week. Where was this going to go anyway? You'll be back in London shortly, and I'm here. Waiting tables and acting in dodgy movies. Maybe . . . oh, I don't know. Your father is obviously keen for you to be with the right woman."

"Freja, I know who you are." He steps forward, his eyes boring deep into my soul. I inhale a shaky breath. "This always felt like more than just a hook-up. Well it did for me." His eyes search mine until I feel so uncomfortable that I look away. "I honestly don't know what happens next, but I do know that I don't ever want to say goodbye."

His admission knocks the air from my lungs. "I don't want you to either."

* * *

I think I feel a little better during the ride back to Santa Monica. Lord Klein's toxicity towards me was shocking and upsetting, but Nate's kindness has been incredible. He is strong, smart and clearly no stranger to his father's power-playing, but given his father clearly detests me, I'm not sure how – or if – this can go anywhere.

We sit in the back seat of the car, our hands entwined as if we've known each other all of our lives. I ask myself if I've fallen in love with him, and my brain apologises and says, "Of course you have."

Oh fuck.

I'm in trouble.

* * *

My cul-de-sac is eerily quiet. The chauffeur drives up to the front yard and Nate tells him to wait. We get out of the car, but when I walk around to his side, he's standing motionless. His eyes are glued to the pavement.

"What is it?" I ask, following his gaze. Then I see what he's looking at and my heart almost implodes inside my ribcage. "Is that . . . is it . . .blood?"

"Get in the car, Freja." Nate doesn't wait for me to respond. He opens the back door of the car, but I don't move. My friends are in that house. "Freja, quickly. Get inside."

"Do you want me to call the cops, Mr Klein?"

asks the chauffeur.

"I'll check it out first," Nate says as I move halfway to the open car door.

"Nate, this isn't England, it's Los Angeles. The bad guys here have guns."

Nate's face pales slightly, but then he shrugs. "Just get in the car, and give me your house key. I'll quickly get the lowdown."

I rummage around in my tote bag for my key and hand it to him. "Nate, I've watched every episode of *24*. When unarmed guys do stuff like this, it never ends well."

"The lady's right, sir," says the chauffeur.

The possible danger registers in Nate's expression and his skin pales. "Fine." He takes his phone out of his pocket. "I'll call the landline first."

We can hear the telephone ringing inside the house. I pray somebody answers, but when the ringing abruptly stops and Nate starts to talk, my heart leaps into my throat and almost chokes me.

"Peyton?" Deep, concerned ridges develop on Nate's forehead and on the bridge of his nose. "Are you okay? . . . Oh my god, what happened? Slowly . . . okay . . ." He ushers me back out of the car. "Have you called someone? Ambulance? Police?" Nate's voice blurs in my eardrums as my pulse thuds in my head. He takes my hand, leads me to the front door and unlocks the door. "We're here now."

I rush into the house behind Nate, my heart pounding as I take in my surroundings. Some of the furniture has been moved. Bloodstained clothing, paper towels and cushions litter the floor . . . and Richie is lying on his side on the sofa. Peyton, in her diner uniform, looks like she's been in a car crash. There's blood on her apron, blood on her hands and blood in her hair. I can't even think straight. "Oh my god, what happened? Are you okay?" I ask Peyton.

"I'm fine, but I can't stop the bleeding." There's a wildness in her eyes that I've never seen before. "He walked through the front door like this. I've gone through so many paper towels . . . It's mainly his lip and his nose."

I kneel on the floor, staring in horror at Richie's bruised and battered face. "Who did this to him?" I take hold of his hand as tears fill my eyes.

Nate kneels down next to me. "Rich, my car's outside. We need to get you to hospital."

Richie shakes his head. "I can't," he says weakly. "No insurance."

"Screw the sodding health insurance." Nate gently moves Richie's head into the light to scan his injuries. "I'll pay for it, whatever it takes."

"No," groans Richie. "No, I'll be okay. It looks worse than it is."

"Don't be so bloody ridiculous," says Nate. "You're covered in bruises. You could have concussion, broken bones . . . anything. Where did this happen?"

"He said two guys jumped him in the street outside," says Peyton. "But he also didn't come home last night and . . . Richie, just tell him."

Richie groans again. He wipes fresh blood from his nose and rolls onto his back. "No."

"I'm going to call the police," says Nate. "This is crazy. What if whoever did this comes back? Freja could be in danger and so could Peyton. And so could Riley." He stands up and I move closer to Richie, holding his hand as carefully yet firmly as I can.

"Don't you get it?" Peyton starts to cry. "This is all your goddamn fault!"

Nate takes a step back, his eyes filled with horror. "What do you mean?"

Richie attempts to speak but only coughs again. I apply pressure to his bleeding lip with some wadded-up paper towels. "Is this about the money?" I ask, already knowing the answer.

"Of course it's about the money," yells Peyton. She places her hands on her hips and attempts to sniff away her tears. "You just straight up asked him for three hundred grand. How the hell did you think he'd be able to find that kind of money?"

Nate hangs his head. "I didn't think he'd be able to find it. I thought we would sell up. Richie said he was fine with that."

"*We* would just sell up? *We*?" She tosses her head back and laughs. "Jesus Christ, I can't believe you're so fucking dumb."

"Peyton, leave it," croaks Richie, attempting to sit up. I put my hands on his chest to ease him back down.

"No, I won't leave it." She wipes at her blotchy face. "This has gone far enough now. While you two were out enjoying yourselves, flirting and fucking and not having a care in the world, Richie was doing everything he could to save his livelihood . . . and his home."

Nate looks at me, and all I can see in his eyes is heartbreak.

"It started with one loan for the theatre six

138

months ago. But then he needed another to cover our rent arrears. Then he borrowed more, and then more, and again, and again. What do you think happens to people who can't pay back the million per cent interest on *those* kind of loans from *those* kinds of people? Richie doesn't have a rich billionaire daddy he can go to for pocket change, but you do. Why did you have to take everything away from him? If they'd have killed him, it would have been your fault."

Both of us are too stunned to speak. Peyton starts sobbing again, but before we can formulate a plan to fix this mess she runs upstairs to her bedroom. I reach for the first aid kit and continue the task of patching up Richie.

"I'll pay for all of this, Rich. We can go to the ER now and we can forget about selling the theatre. I'll get the money I need some other way, or I won't get it at all. It doesn't matter."

Richie bites down hard on his own teeth when I apply antiseptic cream to his cuts, but he still manages to shake his head. "No," he says, his voice fading dimly into a whimper. "Peyton shouldn't have said all that stuff. You've done too much already – you gave me a chance and I blew it."

"I should have given you more time . . . I should have . . ."

"Don't you see?" says Richie. "It wouldn't have made any difference. I'd already fucked my life up."

Nate flops down in an armchair as I start cutting up Band-Aids. His shoulders are hunched and his elbows rest on his knees. He looks like he's working this all through in his head, and for the first time in my entire life, I don't feel like I should offer up unsolicited advice or recommendations. I trust him to do the right thing.

"I'm going to make this okay, Richie," he says as his dark, sorrowful eyes meet mine. "I'm going to make everything okay."

11

SUNDAY WAS SPENT IN THE Good Samaritan Hospital. Nate paid all of Richie's hospital bills, and JJ has taken the day off college to be with him today while I go to work. Peyton has moved in with her parents – temporarily – until we can be certain the house is safe.

"Are you sure you're going to be okay?" I say, opening the front door.

Richie holds his bandaged arm steady with his good hand. His face is so swollen he can barely open his eyes. "I'll be fine. Nate's really helped me out. Not just with the hospital, but with my debts too. I think I'll owe him for the rest of my life."

JJ comes to the door. "Guilt money. You've definitely sold your soul to the devil, big guy."

Richie's demeanour falters and he gives JJ a sharp look. There's something they're not telling me. "Okay, out with it." I place my bag on the floor and fold my arms.

JJ's face falls. "There's nothing," he says, but his eyes are screaming "Oh, shit."

"For Christ's sake, what is it now? The last thing I need is stress and worry on top of having to psych myself up to work naked today."

Richie sighs as if he's holding the weight of the entire planet on his shoulders. "Nate bailed me out with money he got from his father."

"And?" I ask, dreading the inevitable quid pro quo.

Richie shrugs. "And . . . that's it. There's nothing

else."

"So why didn't you tell me?"

"Because you hate him," says JJ.

My brain whirrs. When did I tell JJ – or anybody – about my feelings towards Lord Klein? Have I been sleep talking? Did Nate tell them? I narrow my eyes and study their body language. JJ is twitchy, and Richie's bruised face has paled from purple to lilac. "Bullshit. You're lying to me."

"How do you know?" JJ says. I give him a pointed look and he acquiesces. "Fine. Nate told us not to tell you." Oh, for heaven's sake, why did I think he was different? Why did I have to fall so stupidly in love with him? I can't bear guys being secretive and overly protective. I pick up my tote, swing it over my shoulder and walk out the door. "Wait! What are you going to do?" calls JJ.

"I'm going to work. And I'll be spending all damn day asking myself why the men in my life can't be straight with me."

"You're overreacting," he shouts as I walk down the street to the bus stop.

"No, I'm not."

* * *

After an hour and a half in make-up, I arrive on set. I've spent the last day worrying about Richie, and now I'm angry with Nate. I needed to mentally prepare myself for today – or rather the nakedness of today – but work has barely entered my head.

The scene starts with my character, Maya, waking up in the arms of Todd's character, Drew.

142

Chronologically, it's the morning after the kitchen sex scene that we shot on Friday. We then proceed to have bed sex, followed by shower sex. Hopefully we can get both scenes done and over with today, because that will only leave the rather intense, but ridiculously scripted, sex scene in the Camaro before my character dies. I've never played a corpse before, but it must be very easy money. I sit down in the canvas chair that has my name pinned to it and start reading through my script.

"Have you heard?" asks Todd, taking a seat next to me.

"Heard what?"

"Reed's ass is majorly on the line. He's running over budget, and if he doesn't find more cash there's a real danger the movie will be shelved."

Great. Freaking great. Wouldn't it be just be my luck if, after putting my reputation on the line to film this crappy movie, it never sees the light of day. "Why is it down to Reed to find investors?"

"The head honcho at Twilight was replaced last month and the new guy hates Reed. He's refusing to inject any more of the studio's money in the movie, so if Reed can't raise the cash himself, we're screwed."

"But there's only my scenes left to complete. The studio would be dumb to not see it through."

"They'd view it as cutting their losses. The movie is over budget and over schedule. Losing Anna in the middle of it really hurt us."

I swear to god, if I make it through today only for this movie to end up in Twilight's trashcan, there will be blood. As I watch the crew prepare the bed, I start to feel light-headed with nerves. Filming

143

nude sex scenes may get easier the more often you do them, but they're still the hardest thing about being an actress. Todd is sweet, but he's inexperienced and therefore completely useless at giving me any support.

"So, how are you feeling about today?" asks Todd. It's as if he's reading my mind.

"I've got a knot in my stomach the size of the Grand Canyon and it won't go away."

He laughs. "Me too. They should be supplying us with bourbon instead of mineral water. You didn't, um, reply to my text."

Oh shit, he's right. "I'm so sorry, Todd. I've had a really tough weekend. What was the problem again?"

"Reed doesn't want me to use a you-know-what – the cock sock."

"Oh." I translate Todd's blushes as abject fear of what's to come. "Well, don't worry about it. I'm sure we'll manage." I give his shoulder a friendly nudge.

"Can we have everyone in place?" Reed shouts his orders to the assembled crew members, producers and assistants, and half of them disperse. "We're a closed set today, so anyone without clearance has to leave."

We lose everyone but Reed, camera operator Miguel and three female crew members – an assistant director, script supervisor and sound mixer. A guy called Adrien, who looks like he's still in high school, is doubling up as boom mike operator and key grip. Christy also remains behind to touch up our make-up as needed. I'm thankful to have a friendly face.

"Looks like it's battle stations," I say to Todd.

I stand up and walk over to the bed. He walks over to join me but hangs a few paces behind. His aura is stifling. He nervously twists the rope on his towelling dressing gown. This is going to be one hell of a long day.

"Okay," says Reed, schedule in hand and a blue pen tucked behind his ear. "We're starting in the bed. Todd, I want you behind Freja, spooning her. Marge will arrange the sheet."

I untie my robe, and I'm just about to take it off when Todd stops me. "Wait, I'm not . . . um . . . ready."

Reed swings around. "Oh, for fuck's sake, don't start this again," he says, rubbing at the creases in his brow.

"I'm not . . . I'm just worried. If I lie behind her, touching, then I'm worried about . . ." I can feel the heat radiating from Todd's body. I am a patient person, but I want to grab hold of his shoulders and shake him. "I'd prefer to wear the covering."

"What?" Reed screws up his eyes. "No. We've been through this. Post-production is a fucking nightmare if a guy's wearing one of those things. I don't have the budget for the amount of editing we'd need and it can make great shots totally unworkable. You have to trust me here, Todd. I promise the film will be cut tastefully."

"I trust you to edit out my dick, Reed, but that's not the point. I'm worried about where Freja will be—"

"You mean you're worried you'll get a boner if her ass touches you?" Reed asks. Could he be any blunter? He apologised for his directness on Friday,

145

but it seems he hasn't learned a thing from all the extra hours of filming we had to do because of the state Todd got himself in. "Don't worry about it. Most actors I've worked with get hard during sex scenes. You'll act better if you're aroused anyway, so just go with it. But if you do get one when you're behind her, make sure you stick it somewhere innocuous."

Oh, Jesus Christ, what's wrong with him? "Todd, can we just get on with this please?" I say, dropping my robe from my body. "I don't want a repeat of Friday." I climb onto the bed and lie down on my side. I'm grateful that I got to do the big undress while my brain was preoccupied with being pissed at Todd, but as I wait for Marge to cover me up, the fact that my bare ass is pointing in the direction of the adolescent boom guy makes all the icky butterflies return.

I feel Todd climb onto the bed, but I don't move a muscle in case I unnerve him. His body presses against my back, and then I feel his hand digging around in the space between his groin and my ass. "Oh god, I'm sorry," he says when he touches me for the third time.

"You're fine," I say between gritted teeth, blocking out the very noticeable warm, prodding sensation I'm feeling on my left butt cheek. This is probably going to be the worst day of my life. But at least it will provide me with stories I can entertain my friends with for years to come.

Assistant director Marge is a no-nonsense hard-faced woman in her fifties with straggly grey hair that looks like it's been ripped off a horse's tail and glued onto her head. She artistically arranges the white sheet around my crossed legs and then grabs Todd's hand and places it just under my boob. When she's done she stands back, admires the view and gives Reed the thumbs up.

"Action!"

As soon as I hear the clapperboard, I start "waking up". I try to push the weirdness of Todd groping my breasts out of my head. An image of Nate flashes in my mind, and for the very briefest of seconds, it feels like I'm betraying him to be lying naked in the arms of another guy. I quickly switch on my professional acting head and block out all the icky feels.

We shoot the waking-up scene thirty times before we get it right. I'm ashamed to say most of the extra takes are down to me, not Todd, this time. It takes me just a little bit longer to get to grips with the camera's movements. We move onto scene two later than planned. This involves me saying my lines while lying on my back and staring into Todd's bright blue eyes. I feel his semi making a slow crawl up my stomach as he lies over me and I shudder. Then my mind goes blank. Suzy, the script supervisor, calls out my forgotten line.

"I'm sorry," I say.

"No, it's my fault," says Todd. He flips onto his back, pulling the sheet over his ever-so-slightly erect penis. He hides his bright-red face with his arms.

"Holy shit, Todd. Do you want to take five minutes to sort yourself out?" asks Reed. He's staring at Todd's groin with a measure of amusement, but I'm starting to feel a little bit sick. Adrien, the boom guy, passes Todd his robe. He puts it on and sprints off the set.

I brace myself for yet another apology when Todd returns half an hour later, but he promptly disrobes and gets straight back into the bed.

"Right, guys, seeing as Todd has returned to us without a boner, we'll take the opportunity to film scene three." My stomach plunges to my feet. I was hoping I'd be able to work up to the joyousness of having to sit on Todd's lap and simulate penetrative sex, but it appears not.

Todd gets himself into position while Christy helps me out of my robe. She checks the fabric hasn't removed any of my spray tan and gives my hair a quick brush through. I concentrate on controlling my breathing, but I'm in freefall. My brain is full of thoughts I don't want to think about, my nerves are shot and my entire body has started to shake. I pray I don't vomit up my breakfast.

"Remember you're the most powerful person in this room," Christy whispers as she finishes brushing my long hair. I let her words sink in. They worked for me on Friday, so they should work for me today.

I inhale a deep breath and position myself over Todd's groin, keeping as much space between us as I can.

Reed approaches. "Okay, sugar, I know this is a tough scene, so we're going to take it nice and slow. Don't worry about the number of takes we might need to get it right, and don't worry about where Miguel is pointing the camera. I promise the movements will feel robotic in no time at all, and that's when we'll get our best shot."

He returns to his chair and shouts, "Action".

Pretending to have sex with Todd can be accurately compared to pretending to have sex with a slab of concrete. He's paralysed with fear in case he gets another boner, so he's trained his eyes to stare up at the ceiling instead of at me. On the fifth take, he finally gets his act together with the eye contact, but when Reed orders him to place his mouth on my breast, I feel a very unwelcome stiffening underneath me again. Should I be doing anything to turn him off here? I mean, really! Why did the gods of good fortune cast me opposite a newly divorced guy undergoing a midlife crisis?

"Oh god, I'm so sorry," he says, again. I tell him it's fine, again, but actually, it isn't fine. His random pop-up erections are getting extremely tiresome.

"Action!"

Miguel has the camera trained on me when we start shooting again. I concentrate on elongating my body, tossing my hair back and making all the correct sex sounds. I think I'm getting used to the robotic actions needed to make the scene convincing – just as Reed said – so I put everything I have into it.

Because my focus is entirely trained on Todd, I notice when his attention shifts from me to goings-on at the back of the studio. I sigh inwardly, but as nobody has yelled "Cut", I continue to act. I grab hold of my breasts, teasing my own nipples while Todd's hands move against my hips. Then, out of the corner of my eye, I notice Miguel has stopped looking into his equipment. His olive skin has noticeably reddened, and he has a grave look on his face.

"Cut," yells Marge.

I hear Reed talking with someone . . . who? I turn my head, and a huge, swirling tornado of revulsion almost knocks me to the ground. I turn away from the intruder, my arms covering my boobs and my heart beating so fast I feel like it's about to blast out of my chest.

Todd squirms underneath me, attempting to see what's going on. He looks at me, then he looks at *him*. Then he looks at me again.

But it's Miguel who speaks out. "Who is this?" he says in his husky Mexican accent. "Sir, you cannot come in here."

I close my eyes. I want to cry, scream and run as far away from here as I can, but I'm frozen to the spot. Why is nobody doing anything? My pulse is racing in my head, throat and chest . . . I feel like I'm drowning. Am I in shock? Am I going to pass out? I feel like I could. I feel like I might die.

Reed steps forward. "This is Lord Leonard Klein, and as of this morning he practically owns this movie as the major investor. He's coming on board as an executive producer too, so all of us are working for him."

Todd doesn't bat an eyelid. Adrien, who is kneeling on the bed next to me with a gigantic furry boom mike in his hand, yawns and waits for the camera to start rolling again. Marge looks at her watch and chews on a wad of gum. Nobody cares.

"Okay, Freja, this time we need an orgasm, and I'd like to hear lots of noise. Just let go and belt it out," says Reed.

"I can't do this." My voice is little more than a desperate, panicked whisper. Todd is the only one who hears me. I'm sitting on top of his belly, so when he reaches up to touch my arm he's able to feel how much I'm shaking. I hear the click-clack of Klein's expensive shoes as he walks around the bed. I sense his gaze travelling all over my body, and an ice-cold shiver settles into my spine.

"Well this looks fun," Klein says. His tone is dripping with sarcasm. He sits down in Miguel's chair, crosses his legs and plasters a grin on his face that sets my teeth on edge. "I've always wanted to watch a movie being made."

I drag my hair forward, over my shoulders, in a pathetic attempt to cover myself. Klein's eyes burn through me. Todd tightens his hold on my arm and mouths, "Are you okay?"

Miguel moves to stand between Klein and me. "Reed, it isn't acceptable to have someone without union clearance on a closed set. This puts our actors in a vulnerable position."

"Oh, don't be such a pussy, Miguel. Don't give me any of your PC bullshit," Reed says in a spikey tone. "Now get back in place."

Miguel returns to his position and picks up his camera, his face stiff and serious.

"Action!"

The sound of the clapperboard shoots straight through me. I drop my arms from my chest and start to move, but I can feel Klein's eyes on me. I stop dead still, my body shaking with every breath I take. "I need to get out of here."

"What the hell? Cut!" Reed yells in exasperation. "Freja, for fuck's sake, don't let Todd rub off on you when you've been acting so well. We only have forty minutes before lunch. Please can you just give me one quick orgasm?"

"Oh, I don't think this is *all* Freja's fault." Lord Klein sits forward in the chair. "This is a demanding role. Freja's character's sole purpose in this film is to trap poor old Todd here, so unless she has experience of ensnaring men from which she can draw, it's going to be tough for her."

Reed clears his throat. "Um, okay. I don't think that's the problem here, but okay. Are we ready to roll again? Miguel?"

"No, we're not ready." Miguel places his equipment down on the dolly and squares off against Reed. "This isn't right. We have a duty to make sure actors feel safe on set."

Marge steps forward too. She deliberately blocks Klein's view of me with her wide hips and baggy jeans. She puts her hand on my shoulder. "Do you need to take five minutes, honey?"

I nod my head. Christy brings me my robe and assists me in wrapping it tightly around my body, then both women help me climb off Todd.

Without a word, I shuffle off the bed and go to my trailer. Christy comes with me. My head is spinning faster with every second that passes, and as soon as I get inside to safety, my stomach starts heaving on bile. I rush to the toilet and throw up.

"Freja, are you okay in there, honey?" says Christy.

I make a soft groaning noise, then I flush. I drag myself off the floor, my legs wobbling beneath me like a newborn foal's. I go to the bedroom and curl up into a ball on the bed.

Christy sits down next to me. "Do you know that guy?"

I push my damp hair off my face. My skin is cool and clammy. "I'm dating his son, and two days ago he warned me off. He said some stuff that got under my skin and I hate him for it."

The make-up artist scoots closer and places a comforting hand on my leg. "Freja, this is crazy. Are you telling me he has invested hundreds of thousands of dollars in this movie as some kind of sick power trip?"

"Yes." Hearing Christy verbally process what Klein has done makes it all the more horrific. "How was he able to walk onto set like that? Why . . . ?" Nausea rises into my throat again. Why didn't I say something to him? Why didn't I rise up, like I always do, and put him in his place? "I'm not ashamed of who I am, so I shouldn't have reacted like that. He was sending me a message. He was showing me I'm not good enough."

Christy's dark eyes sparkle with rage. "Don't you dare say that about yourself! The guy is as shady as fuck, and what he's just done in there is nothing short of abuse."

Was it abuse? I know I feel like he's invaded my body as well as my mind. He's also made me sick to my stomach.

"Are you going to tell the guy you're seeing?"

I shake my head. "I don't want to be the catalyst for destroying his relationship with his father. His family has a name and a legacy and I don't understand any of it, but it must be important."

"None of that matters, Freja. The only thing you need to remember is you've done absolutely nothing wrong, while Lord Fucking Voldemort back there has spent a fuckload of cash in order to intimidate you. You should be calling the cops on his creepy ass."

"It isn't against the law to invest in a movie, Christy." I get up and start to get dressed. "I can't do this anymore. I'm not going back on set."

"Oh my god, really?" says Christy. "Are you sure? It would be such a shame. You've done some really great work already."

I pull my t-shirt over my head and start putting on my skinny jeans. "I don't care about work, I only care about me. I'm not allowing that man to own a piece of me."

I stuff all my belongings into my tote. I don't need time to think about this. I trust my gut – my intuition – and it's telling me to walk.

I give Christy a hug. "Thanks for everything . . . and I'm sorry. Tell Todd I'm sorry."

"You've nothing to be sorry about," she says. "Just go home. I'll let everyone know."

12

I DON'T WANT TO GO home. I can't handle Richie being disappointed that I'd walked away from the money I promised him. I also can't face telling him I won't be able to pay the extra rent. I feel like a coward – I am a coward. But I also know I need some time to process everything that's happened to me and make sense of it.

"I came as quickly as I could."

Nate sits down next to me. The bench at the end of Santa Monica Pier is the same one we sat on last week. He sweeps one arm around my shoulders while the other grips my waist. We kiss and it's wonderful, but when he leans in to deepen it, I pull away. I leave my fingers lingering on his lips as a rush of intense emotion floods my mind. I don't want to lose him. I don't want to break his heart.

"Hey, what's wrong?" he asks, pulling me into his arms again.

I've had over an hour to plan what I'm going to say, but I'm still not entirely sure if I should be telling him at all. "I walked off my movie and I'm not going back."

"Did something bad happen?" His eyes frantically search mine, and I'm totally blindsided by how much he cares. This thing we have keeps throwing up moments that shock the hell out of me and I still can't believe it's real. How have I fallen in love with someone so quickly and so completely?

My eyes flood with tears. "This isn't me. I don't get scared and I never, ever give up on something important to me, but I just can't . . ."

He takes hold of my hand. "Freja, you're really frightening me."

"I'm sorry. I'm okay, but I'm just not feeling too great about myself. Something happened today that threw me."

He sighs. "You don't have to worry. My dad told me."

Okay, I wasn't expecting that. "He told you?"

"Yeah, he said he wanted to make amends."

"Wait a minute." I rub at my brow. I'm starting to get a killer headache. "What exactly did he tell you?"

"He said he was sorry for checking out your past, and for being rude to you, so he invested in your movie. He said there were financial difficulties. Is this why you quit? Because I'm really sorry if it is."

I just stare at him open-mouthed as he talks. For a split second, I wonder if the relayed information is actually the truth. Did Lord Klein invest in the movie by way of an apology? *Don't be so damn naïve, Freja.* "Didn't it strike you as a bit of an odd move?"

Nate frowns, his beautiful face suddenly racked with suspicion. "It did, but I guess I was pleased. He admitted he'd behaved badly, which he never does, so I was happy he wanted to do something nice for someone I care about."

A tear falls down my face, then another. I try to hold back, but I can't because I know I'm going to break his heart. "That isn't why . . . Fuck . . ." I pull my hand away from his, lean forward and bow my head. Why does loving someone have to be this fucking complicated? I attempt to order my thoughts by focusing on the soft ocean waves as they roll onto the beach.

Nate leans forward too, but I daren't meet his gaze. I don't want to start blubbing again. "What aren't you telling me?" he asks wearily.

I rearrange my words in the right order, then I take a deep breath. "Your father invested in my movie to send me a message. He doesn't want us together and he's made it abundantly clear he doesn't consider me a good match for you."

His body stiffens. "Why would he think that?"

"Because of what I do."

He stands up and grips the metal railing that lines the edge of the pier in front of us. The beach below is busy with surfers, swimmers and sun-worshippers, but just as I did earlier, Nate seems to find comfort in the calmness of the ocean.

"You never asked me about the movie. Richie and JJ told me they didn't want me to do it. Peyton outright accused me of selling myself. But you didn't ask me any questions. Why?"

"Truth?" he asks, his gaze locked on the horizon. "I don't understand the film industry, but I figured if you needed my opinion on your movie you'd ask for it. You know yourself and, jeez, sometimes I think you know *me* better than I know myself. I trusted you'd work within your own comfort zone."

Could he be any more perfect? "I appreciate that," I tell him. "But your father comes from a whole different world. He sees things differently."

Nate turns around and rests against the barrier. He folds his arms and shakes his head. "I don't

157

accept that. My father has been around the block more times than I know about. There are rumours he cheated on my mother, and I know he's cheated on my stepmother on at least two occasions. He's in no place to look down on you for anything."

"My dad lives in a wooden shack with a menagerie of animals, and I don't have a penny to my name. I wait tables that I hate and I audition for acting roles I never get. I'm not ashamed of who I am, but if your father superficially compares me to someone like Evelyn, I'm always going to come up short."

"But I don't love Evelyn, I love you!"

I think my heart has stopped beating. I bite the inside of my cheek to check if I'm still alive. "You love me?"

His sunshine grin returns for the first time in days. "Yeah, I love you. I am *in* love with you. Completely. Wildly. You take my breath away, and then you remind me to breathe."

He sits back down next to me and I want to be teleported to the moon. There's a huge achy ball of something scary ballooning in my chest and it hurts and I don't want it to be there. "Um . . . okay."

He laughs softly. "Is that all you have to say?"

"I don't know. I don't think I want you to love me."

His jaw tenses. His expression is hard and his eyes fill with anguish. "Why not?"

"Because of what happens next. How are we going to give each other up?"

"If you mean when I go home, then you need to know I'm already home." He reaches out and tucks a tendril of hair behind my ear. "Look at me," he says, gently turning my face towards him. "Home isn't four brick walls and a front door. Home is you. I'm not tied to London. Are you tied to LA?"

I shake my head. "No, not now that I've blown my acting career."

"We can go anywhere: New York, London, Hong Kong . . . anywhere. This could be your next great spontaneous adventure."

I can't stop a huge grin taking hold of my face. "We've known each other a week, Nate. This is a little too close to love at first sight. Walt Disney-style love at first sight."

He quirks an eyebrow. "If you're accusing me of falling in love with you during Mickey and Minnie's burlesque show, then you're absolutely spot on."

"Really?" I laugh. "So you're saying you fell in love at first sight with my tits?"

"No, I'm saying I fell in love with your confidence, then your humour, then finally I fell in love with your heart."

He takes my hand and I realise that *this* is what I've always needed. It wasn't hot-chocolate walks in the forest with a nice, stable guy. I didn't need someone who would tame me or ground me. I've only ever needed someone to hold my hand and tell me they love me. I look around briefly, then I crash my lips against his. He responds by strengthening the kiss, his hands wrapped up in my hair. I don't care that the pier is crowded with hundreds of people, but when he pulls away with a nervous giggle, I figure he does.

"We may need to get a room," I say with a laugh.

His smile is so breathtakingly beautiful that I

have to summon the strength of a herd of elephants to stop myself jumping on top of him and showering him with more kisses. Instead, I snuggle up close, my back against his chest, my body enveloped in his strong arms.

"Freja." My name floats softly on his breath as he strokes my hair. "I don't want you to worry about my father anymore."

"I don't want to come between you, Nate, but investing in my movie wasn't an act of kindness on his part. Same with paying off Richie's loan sharks. This is all about controlling people's lives to get what *he* wants."

"I know," he says, his fingers gliding through my hair. "He's already asked Richie to sing his praises with Aaron. That's how badly he wants to win."

"And he always does win. He knows how to wield power."

"He does, but I don't understand what he gets out of playing power games with your movie." Nate brings my head into the crook of his neck. I feel so safe locked in his arms, but my stomach is churning bile.

I pull his arm closer around my body and grip it tighter. "We were shooting on a closed set. There was a skeleton crew who were all vetted and had clearance to be there. Some of the scenes were really difficult – for me and the guy I was acting with."

"You mean sex scenes?" he asks tenderly.

"Yes, and I was completely naked. We both were."

"Oh, I see." He kisses the top of my head protectively. "Well, I guess sometimes you have to

160

do stuff like that, right?"

"Exactly. No actress enjoys doing sex scenes. It's weird and you're worried out of your mind about the logistics of where your ass is pointing half the time, but you just accept it's required in some roles and you get on with it." I move out of his hold, because I need to see his face. "Except this time I couldn't do it."

"Why? Because you found out my dad had invested?"

"No, because your dad came onto the set, without clearance, and watched me."

Heat immediately explodes onto his face, and his body shoots forward. His eyes are alight with rage. "He did what?"

"He just appeared there . . . and I couldn't do anything . . ." Revulsion claws at my throat as I watch Nate struggle to process what I'm telling him. "He wouldn't leave, so I had to."

Nate leaps to his feet. He grips the pier railings hard, until his knuckles are the same colour as the single cloud in the sky above us. "Let me get this straight. My father invaded a film set where you were naked, and vulnerable . . . why? In order to do what?"

I stand up next to him. His skin is aflame and a river of sweat trails the angry vein that has appeared along the side of his face. "It was a game. He was letting me know that he is far more powerful than me." Nate grits his teeth, and the full horror of what happened to me this morning hits me full blast in the centre of my chest. "Please say something."

"I . . . can't. I don't know what to say. All I can think about is ending that bastard's life and how

161

many different, excruciating ways I can think of to do it."

I flinch at the violence in his words. "I'm sorry this has hurt you. I wish I hadn't told you. I didn't know what to do."

He grabs hold of my shoulders. "I'm not letting him get away with this. You should finish your movie. I'll make sure he doesn't go anywhere near you ever again. I promise."

I cover one of his hands with mine. His skin is burning hot, the result of too much sun and too much rage. "I meant it when I said I wasn't going back on set. I can't do it knowing your father owns the movie now."

He starts to move away, taking my hand with him, and he sends me some sunshine. "You want to live – and so do I, and we could do it together. Say you'll come with me."

"Where to?"

"To start the next chapter of our lives."

* * *

Nate bursts into the Chateau Room of the Beverly Wilshire. I'd hoped he would calm down during the ride over, but as soon as we got out of the car, it was like all the rage and hurt slammed back into him. The solid wooden door crashes back against the wall.

"You piece of shit," he yells, rounding on his father. He walks around the table and is on him in three strides. "We're through. I'm resigning from Klein & Co, I'm going to start up on my own and

I'm going to move heaven and earth to be with the woman I love."

Oh, Jesus Christ. My blood pressure soars as eight pairs of eyes fall upon me. Sam rises to stand between his warring brother and father. Aaron puts his head in his hands.

Nate turns to Aaron. "Don't sign with him. My father deliberately tanked Joyco's stock to cheat you, and he has a company in India already signed up to make your product at a fraction of the cost he's claiming in the buyout deal. All he cares about is winning, and he'll stuff anybody – partner, client, friend or family – to get what he wants." He leaves his father's side to stand next to me. "You're special to Freja, therefore you're special to me. I know how to market your product, and I want to do it in partnership with you. I'll set up shop anywhere: China, Singapore, Korea, the States – anywhere. Just don't let him cheat you."

Aaron looks from Nate to me and back again. His lawyer whispers something in his ear, but Lord Klein catches their glances and ups the ante. "Fifty per cent on top of what I originally offered."

Cuthbert Ashby, Klein's partner, clears his throat. "We can't go that high, Leonard. Not without consulting the shareholders."

"Screw the shareholders," bellows Lord Klein. "They do as *I* say, not the other way around."

Aaron reclines back in his chair. He reaches for a pen. My heart leaps, thinking he's going to sign some document or other, but he just turns the pen around and around between his fingers.

"You need to think this through, Aaron," I say.

"We could really use the money, Freja," he

replies. I feel selfish. This amount of money could set Aaron and JJ up for life. I trust Nate a million times more than I trust his father, but he doesn't have a company, or the finances and contacts his father has.

"What a surprise," says Lord Klein. "I should have expected Miss Larsen would have something to do with this."

"You bet your life she does," says Nate, reaching for my hand. "I've got to hand it to you though. I completely fell for your bullshit. I believed you when you said you invested in Freja's movie to make up for all the shitty things you said and did to her."

"Oh, yes." Klein's grey eyes turn steely as an unnerving smile sweeps across his face. "There was absolutely no truth in that."

Nate grips my hand tighter. "What the hell did you think I'd do when I found out about this morning?"

Lord Klein either has the best poker face I've ever seen or he genuinely doesn't give a shit. "You mean, when I checked in on my investment?"

"I mean when you invaded Freja's privacy."

"Privacy?" he says, his voice laced thick with sarcasm. "Is that what you call taking your clothes off in front of a room full of people and pretending to fuck somebody? That studio was full of crew members this morning, and when the film is shown, the entire world will be invading her so-called privacy."

"I won't be finishing the film," I say, holding my head high. "I've already informed Reed McHale."

"Then you'll be sued for breach of contract."

Nate laughs. "No she won't. The film studio had a legal responsibility to keep their employees safe, so her contract had already been broken by you."

"Don't be so melodramatic. She was hardly in any danger, Nathaniel." Klein rises to his feet and glares across the boardroom table at his son. "And it's actually quite laughable you're suggesting that I, as opposed to the penis she was sitting on, was a threat to her safety."

It's as if a match has been lit. "What the fuck are you insinuating?" roars Nate. He strides forward but then stops, silently locking horns with his father. But a fire has been ignited inside of me too. My heartbeat thuds in my chest and rings in my ears. I hate this man more than I've ever hated anybody in my entire life, and if I could get away with it, I'd happily punch him in the face. Repeatedly. While wearing a spikey glove.

"I'm not insinuating anything, Nathaniel. I'm very plainly stating a fact."

Nate looks at me with something in his eyes that I've never seen there before – shame and regret. Klein is making my acting role sound terrible. Was it terrible? No. *Min Gud, Freja, stop!* Why am I letting him do this? "Far bigger-named actresses than me film the exact same kind of scenes for blockbuster movies every single day."

Evelyn glances at me, and I see an encouraging smile appear on her face. I wasn't expecting that. I was expecting the same expression that I'm seeing on her father's face. Cuthbert looks as though he has a very unpleasant smell lingering under his nose.

"What did you hope to gain from this, Dad?"

165

Nate asks.

"You're a Klein and you're my eldest son," he says. "You have a bright future ahead of you, and I have a legacy to protect. I'm not going to let you risk your future on a gold-digger."

"How dare you!" I yell, refusing to watch my words any longer. "I've barely known Nate for one week. I haven't asked him for anything, and I never will. I wouldn't care if he was stone broke – in fact I'd prefer it that way, because then he would be free to live his life unburdened by you. You're a rope around his neck, a power-mad sociopath incapable of basic human empathy, love or respect. What you did today was terrible – really terrible – and I swear to god, if you come anywhere near me ever again I will make it my life's mission to destroy you." Boiling-hot blood sloshes in my veins, but I don't flinch or stammer or shake. This man is going to find out that he can't intimidate me or threaten me or do anything that will make me doubt myself ever again. "You're going to learn that you can't control me."

I turn my back to him. I walk over to where Nate is standing and gently touch his arm. I see a faint ghost of sunshine trying to break through the clouds. "I'm done here," I say to him.

"I'm done too," he replies.

"Me too," says Aaron, his voice raised confidently. He shoves a bundle of papers across the table in Lord Klein's direction, then he and his lawyer walk over to join us. "I like the idea of keeping some involvement in bringing Dave to market. I think we could have a great time doing this." He offers his hand and Nate enthusiastically shakes it.

"Welcome aboard," he says.

All four of us leave the stifling room. My excitement and my sense of setting the world to rights is palpable. I feel like I actually am on my way to having the life I need and want – and yes, it's with champagne. We could make this work – all of us – together.

13

WHEN I WAKE, I'M WRAPPED up in Nate's protective arms. My body is moulded against his as if we're two parts of the same whole – "the One". I've never been one of those people who believe there's just one special person out there – a soulmate – that we should spend our lives trying to find. I've always thought there were lots of possible soulmates for everyone, and their suitability changes for us as we grow. Sometimes, like with Per, we grow in different directions, breaking apart when there's nothing left to bind us together. Other times, we grow together, in the same direction, and that's when love lasts.

I'll admit that this was always just Freja's Very Unscientific Philosophy for why some relationships fizzle out. I've never believed in fate. There's no cosmic force bringing destined souls together. But as I nestle against Nate's hard body, breathing in the fresh, breezy scent of his cologne that lingers on my skin as well as his, I know he is "the One". He gets me and I get him. Nate isn't anything like the guys at college, or dates I've met at bars. What we have isn't just different than what I had with Per, it seems *more*. Can you have more than love? It sounds ridiculous, of course, and maybe it is, but I don't know how else to describe it.

"You're awake," he purrs sleepily against my cheek.

"I am." I snuggle against him, loving the feel of every inch of his skin as it melts into mine.

"How long have you being watching me sleep?"

"Not long."

His fingers drum against my spine, then he kisses me softly. His lips are dry and cracked from yesterday's sun-drenched afternoon on the beach. We celebrated with JJ and Aaron, then we all had dinner at the High Rooftop Lounge. "I'm going to miss you today."

My heart sinks. "Yeah, me too, but you have exciting stuff to do. I'm so happy for you and Aaron. JJ is too. I can't believe everything has turned out for the best."

He kisses me again. "And it's only going to get better. I've got a fabulous project I can really sink my teeth into, and a new business partner." I smile, but I also feel sad. His venture is taking him back to England in three days. He sits up slightly, propping himself up on his elbow. "Wu Chong is only in London until next week. I wish I could stay here with you, but I can't miss the chance to see him. Baifu Technology is making great waves in the tech world, and I need to move fast given my funds are being rapidly depleted and I have to find investors immediately."

"What do you mean? I thought you wanted to use your mother's money."

Nate shakes his head. "I can't ask Richie to sell the theatre."

I shudder as my mind returns to last week. I was so angry with Nate for even considering forcing Richie to sell up, but now I completely understand why he did. "Do you have any other options?"

His smile is wide and beautiful, but it doesn't reach his eyes. "A few. Don't worry about it though. I'll work something out. I always do."

I reach up to stroke his cheek. I feel the soft warmth of his skin under my fingertips and I want to video this moment and keep it forever. I touch his strong jaw until his eyes finally smile. He catches my hand and kisses the inside of my wrist.

"I'll miss you," he says.

"Do you know how long you'll be away?"

"Hopefully no longer than a month, but there's talk of going to China. I'll do everything I can to come back, even if it's just for a weekend, but I wanted to ask . . . do you think you'd be able to come out to London too? I'll pay for your flights, of course."

I hesitate for a moment. I don't feel comfortable with him paying for me, but I'm as poor as a church mouse whose cheese company has just filed for bankruptcy. If the alternative is not seeing him, then there's no other way. "I'd love to go to London. I've never been."

"Haven't you?" One of his hands begins to wander under the sheet.

"No, I learned English in school, then college, but I wasn't fluent until I moved to LA."

"Wow," he says. "You're more foreign than I realised."

"*Tak . . . jeg tror.*" I start to laugh. "What on earth does that mean?"

"It means you're exotic." He finds one of my nipples and gently rolls it between his thumb and forefinger. A moan escapes my mouth and lands on his lips. "And fascinating." He pulls the sheet away

170

from my body. "And the most alluring, incredible, brilliant woman I've ever met."

He places tender, slow kisses on my mouth as his hands travel across my body. It's different to all the times before. The first time we made love was wild, as if we were in competition to be the most captivating sex partner the other had ever had. The second time introduced strawberries and naughtiness, then last night's multiple sessions incorporated positions that would make the Kama Sutra sit up and take notice.

But this time is completely different to those times. There's no fun or kink or explosive passion. Instead there's a quiet, almost overwhelming connection – a rabbit hole I've fallen into that has consumed me completely.

Nate holds my gaze when he enters me, and it's as if he's transferring his soul directly into mine. He is silent, but his eyes are sending me the message that he loves me, needs me and doesn't want to lose me.

I wrap my leg around his hip as he rocks inside me, slowly building up a gentle rhythm. There's no ferocity or urgency this time. Instead every move is being made to steadily increase my pleasure.

"God, I love you," he whispers against my neck as his thrusts become harder. He grips my ass and pushes himself farther into my body. Moans mix with ragged breaths as I take in every wonderful inch of him.

"I love you too," I murmur against his cheek.

"That's the first time you've said that," he says with a smile that makes his whole body glow.

"I was waiting for the right time."

Moments later his breathing begins to flow in stronger waves and his thrusts become more frenzied. I grip the back of his neck as he empties into me, holding him close as he says my name, accompanied by another "I love you."

* * *

I was hoping to spend the rest of the afternoon catching up with friends. I haven't seen Dana and Marie for over a week, and I know they'll be dying to hear all about Nate – particularly Dana, whose life depends on how happy her friends are. When Katrina and Joe became an item she ate so much celebratory ice cream that she put on nine pounds.

But, after organising a meet-up, my plans are cruelly halted when I get a desperation text from Todd Warner complete with begging, pleading and yet more apologising. I feel bad. Not bad enough to go back and finish the movie, but bad enough to realise that my choice has impacted on his career and he deserves an explanation.

When I arrive at Twilight Studios, I head straight for my trailer. I have no idea if they're shooting on set or on location today, but Todd said he'd come to see me as soon as he gets a break. I text Christy to let her know I'm here, but she replies that she resigned this morning after an argument with Reed. She says I gave her the impetus to do what she's always wanted to do, and that's to set up her own mobile beauty salon. I'm so happy for her I could burst.

Time ticks by. Over an hour playing Snake has

drained my cell battery, so I switch it off to preserve the remaining three per cent. If my trailer was suddenly invaded by ghosts, I'd need at least three per cent of battery to get through to Ghostbusters.

I pull a magazine out of my bag and catch up on some celebrity gossip. As I flick through actor interviews, I make a mental note to stop watching *Grey's Anatomy* and *Scrubs*. I've wasted far too much of my life drooling over hot pretend doctors when the stark reality of being a penniless Dane living in America means I can't afford health insurance. If I get sick, I die.

And then there's a knock at my door. Finally!

I jump up off my seat, yank the metal door handle and . . .

What the hell?

"Todd is busy, so I said I'd come to talk to you." Lord Klein walks up the steps to my door with a bottle of wine in his hand.

"I don't want to be rude, but it's three in the afternoon and I'd rather grow a rat's tail out of my ass than share a drink with you. Please leave."

Klein gives me a dark glare. "I have something to say and it can take as long as you want it to take, but I'm not going until I've said it."

"If you don't leave right now, I'm going to call security."

He uncorks the bottle and rolls his eyes. "I own security."

I stand at the door as Klein opens my top cupboards and finds two glasses. Is he for real? "Give me one good reason why I shouldn't walk out that door right now."

"Oh, don't be so dramatic." The agitation in his

gravelly voice is palpable. With his back to me, I hear him pour the wine into the glasses. "Two minutes, that's all I ask."

I hesitate. Revulsion crawls over my skin, but I don't want to give the man power over me, so I push the emotion away and front him out. "Okay, two minutes. And you better start with an apology."

He sits down on the seat and pushes one of the glasses across the table towards me. I sit down in a chair opposite him, but I don't pick up the glass. The last thing I want to do is have a drink with him. "I tend not to apologise, but I'll cut to the chase," he says. He unbuttons his suit jacket and crosses his legs. For some reason I'm drawn to his shoes. They're an unusual shade of brown and ridiculously shiny. It's like he's hollowed out the insides of two giant cockroaches and sunk his feet into them. "How much money will it take for you to eject yourself from my son's life?"

My throat is suddenly so dry that I'm desperate for a drink. I knock back a mouthful of wine. "I told you before. I'm not interested in Nate's money."

"I'm not talking about Nate's money, I'm talking about mine."

He takes a piece of folded paper – a cheque – from his top pocket and hands it to me. Holy shit! I scan the trailer for a video camera. "Is this a joke?"

"No, it's half a million dollars. What could you do with that? Buy your friend's theatre? Or a house with a beach view?"

I stare into his cold eyes and rip up the cheque. "You honestly think I'm that much of a threat?"

Lord Klein leans forward slightly. He isn't ruffled, but there's a discernable urgency in his

174

expression and I sense desperation. He thinks he's losing his son, and he is. His dark olive skin is beaded with sweat. "I don't know if Nathaniel has told you about his mother?" His eyes glance quickly in my direction, awaiting my response. I nod my head. "Pauline was killed in a car crash with the man she was having an affair with. Both of them had high traces of heroin and alcohol in their blood. He swerved at high speed into oncoming traffic. She was decapitated on impact, and her lover died in hospital ten days later. They took five innocent people with them."

Nausea shoots to my throat as he speaks. There isn't a trace of emotion in his voice, so my empathy is for Nate, not for him. "That's terrible. But why are you telling me this?"

"Pauline's mother was a stage actress who married the son of a princess. Aside from the immense difference in class, there are some similarities between you and her. Pauline always wanted to pursue the stage, but it wasn't to be. I think that's what first attracted Nathaniel to you. He took his mother's death hard, and now, seventeen years later, I believe he's projecting his loss onto you."

He's making Nate sound like freaking Norman Bates. "I'm sure that isn't the case."

"You can be sure all you like, but you've only known Nathaniel a few days. I know he's charming, good-looking, wealthy – the dictionary definition of a great catch for a girl like you, but he comes with a vast back catalogue of troubles. He was expelled twice from his boarding school, I had to bail him out of trouble at university more times than I can count, and he racked up six figures in debt when he lived in LA. Has he told you any of this?"

I lie. "Some of it, but I fail to see why—"

"The last time I dug him out of a hole, it was on the condition he worked for me and helped me maintain our family's legacy. Nathaniel's a natural leader. He has a brilliant mind, but he's unfocussed, so I need to keep a watchful eye on him. Pauline's indiscretions came close to destroying all of us. I've been shunned from social events, I've had paparazzi camp out on my front garden, and my sons were bullied mercilessly at school. I'm used to protecting my family from scandals." He slides his suit jacket off his arms and lays it neatly on the seat next to him.

"Again, I don't see what this has to do with me."

"You convinced Nathaniel to resign his position."

A quiet laugh escapes my throat. "No, he made that decision before he met me."

Klein's face remains unreadable, but his eyes register a truth he'd probably never considered. How can he be so proud of his son, yet think he'd jump at my command? "You steered the ship. You orchestrated the situation with Aaron Goodwin, and you couldn't wait to tell him about my checking in on your little movie."

"You seriously think all this happened because of me?" I start to feel light-headed, but I don't know whether it's the heat, the wine or the ridiculous amount of bullshit that is being spewed from this cretin's mouth.

"You encouraged him. He barged into my meeting yesterday, because of you."

"I think you'll find he did that because of *you*. Not me."

"I beg to differ. You're obnoxious and you have too high an opinion of yourself. You're not good enough for my son, so you're going to disappear. Name your price."

The light-headedness spreads from my head to my neck. I rub at my face, wondering why my cheeks feel like they're on fire after only half a glass of wine. "I can't be bought, sir."

"Well that's going to make things very difficult for me." He cocks his head to one side. He's watching me intently, but I can't speak because I can barely keep my eyes open. It feels like my arms are made of rubber and my legs are made of lead. "Just let it happen," he says.

Red-hot heat journeys from my neck to the centre of my chest. My brain is spinning inside my skull. What did he just say? "Let it happen"? I push my hair off my face and try to concentrate on something – anything. My eyes find the tabletop. The metal edge glistens under the ceiling light, then my line of vision travels to the wine glass.

The wine glass.

What has he done?

Every beat my heart makes is accompanied by a stomach lurch. I try to walk, but my legs won't hold me up. I crash against the kitchen benches.

"Sit down, or you'll hurt yourself," he says coldly. "I told you to just let it happen."

I clutch the edge of the kitchen counter. It feels like I'm hanging off a cliff edge.

There are reflections I don't recognise in the shadows of the metal sink . . .

Strange shapes.
My orange-red reflection.
Then black.

14

I FEEL LIKE I'M FLOATING. I can't feel my legs or my arms. My body feels like it's melting into my surroundings – walls, floors, ceiling. I feel tugging and I hear voices. I can't open my eyes, I can't move, I can't speak.

Am I sick?

Am I dreaming?

* * *

There's heaviness all over me. It's pressing me down, dragging me back into the darkness.

Then suddenly the weight is gone.

But I can't even open my eyes.

There's a bright flash. And another. And another.

Then it's black again.

* * *

I don't know what is real. The noise – the voices – sound like they're part of a dream. The tugging and prodding feels real, but maybe it's not. My skin is cold, but my flesh is burning.

Am I sick after all? Am I in a hospital?

The voices grow louder and stronger, but I don't hear words, just a muffled rumble. Quarrelling. The hard sounds collide with each other and flow into a steady hum which invades my ears and fills all the space in my head.

Should I be scared? I don't feel scared. I just feel tired.

I can't raise my head or open my eyes.

So, I choose to sleep.

* * *

A cold blast of outdoor air accompanies a tinny bang. More tugging. More flashing lights.

Hands touching . . . moving me . . . footsteps on a squeaky floor. There's softness under me and warmth around me, but an icy hardness is still biting into my skin, making it raw.

I try to open my eyes, summoning every ounce of strength I possess, until finally I see colours and shapes. Movements. Panic grips me. A dark, terrifying fear builds rapidly in my gut, but there's still a calm energy oozing through my veins. I open my mouth to shout, but my voice dies on just one breath. I try to speak again, but the sound doesn't come.

There's a face I don't know. And a body I don't recognise. He's holding me . . . touching me . . .

I don't want to be touched and I don't want to be held.

More voices. More flashes.

I can't scream.

* * *

It's quiet now. I'm covered with a blanket, so I'm no longer cold – except for a space between my neck and my shoulder blades. I try to move the blanket higher, but my arms are still heavy. I'm in my trailer, not a hospital. I don't feel sick, I don't feel anything at all. Just heaviness.

* * *

It's dark when I open my eyes again. I can see muted shapes and colours – dark blue shadows against charcoal, all lit with shards of silver light. I can move my arms now, but I'm still so tired. I cocoon myself in the blanket. Soft, floating waves of energy drift from my toes to my fingertips. My body feels like it's gliding on air, tranquillity trickling out of every pore.

* * *

I wake with a jolt. I have a pain in my stomach – an urgent, aching pain that takes my breath away. I don't remember where I am at first. I don't know or care how I got here – but I need to go to the bathroom.

My legs feel like they're made of wood. I move one, but the other is dead. I rise up on my elbows and roll myself off the bed. Thankfully my legs come with me. I land in a heap on the floor, and at some point between crawling from the bedroom to throwing up in the toilet, I realise I'm naked.

Hot, burning vomit rockets up from my stomach and scorches my throat as it rushes out of my body. My stomach clenches with every involuntary heave and shudder. When I stop vomiting, I start screaming, and I don't stop screaming until my throat is dry. A searing pain in my head replaces the pain in my stomach. It feels like my brain is getting thrown against my skull, and the only thing I can do to ease the pain, and to ease the intense dizziness, is to curl up into a ball on the freezing-cold floor of the bathroom.

* * *

Hours pass. I'm fairly sure I fell asleep again. Or maybe I passed out. A faint golden light crackles through the bubbly glass of the square bathroom window above me. It's quiet, aside from the squawks of seagulls and the occasional rumbling noise of traffic driving past the studio back lot.

It takes five uncomfortable minutes for me to stand up. I stumble back into the bedroom and mindlessly start putting on my clothes. I can't think about it yet. I don't want to think about it, so I block out. Every time my mind throws up a dreamlike memory – the flashes, the tugging, the voices – I force the agonising thoughts and questions out of my head, but I still feel them nagging at the base of my skull.

When I'm dressed, I search for my cell phone. I need to know how long I was here. My vision is blurry, so it takes me several seconds to check, then double and triple check that I'm seeing what I think

I'm seeing. Six a.m. This means I've lost fifteen hours. The questions flood in on a tidal wave of horror and confusion and I allow my brain to respond with answers. I'm not sick, I was drugged. Nate's father was here. I know he did it, but why? And who else was here? Who was that guy? What did they do to me?

I go to the toilet again. My body is shaking and my stomach feels like it's been crushed and tied into a knot, but I need to know if they've hurt me. I sit down and check over myself. There's nothing. It doesn't hurt anywhere down there. There's no blood and there would be blood if I'd been assaulted, right? There'd be cuts or bruises, – evidence to prove a crime – but there's nothing. I allow relief to wash over me, but a swarm of unyielding worries soon flood back, attacking my mind like a volley of poisoned arrows. Could they have hurt me and left no physical sign of it? If I wasn't assaulted, why did I wake up naked? He wouldn't drug me, remove my clothes and do nothing . . . unless he just wanted to mess with my head. Was that it? Was his only goal to make me feel degraded, confused and ashamed?

This is not happening. It can't be happening. It just can't . . .

Why did I let him into my trailer? Why was I so stupid?

I look at my phone again. My vision is still blurry, but this time it's through tears as well as the after-effects of the drugs. My battery is creeping closer to death and I have six missed calls from Nate and three messages. He wanted to see me last night. He says he's in San Francisco with Aaron today and he's booked flights to go back to London on Friday. He asks if he's done something to upset me, because I haven't answered his calls.

I fall back against the wall. I feel like I'm drowning. Every breath hurts my throat and every thought blasts waves of panic through my body.

I'm going to lose him.

Oh my god, I've already lost him.

I know I've already lost him.

* * *

I take a taxi to a random 24-hour medical clinic in downtown LA. I didn't want to see my regular doctor. The thought of sharing this with him makes my blood run cold, for reasons I don't fully understand. The fear of not being believed, or of being blamed, is just as terrifying a prospect as finding out I could have been hurt in the worst way imaginable. I know this is wrong thinking. This wasn't my fault – I didn't ask for it or deserve it. I don't know why it happened and I don't even know *if* it happened – but I can't tell anybody who knows me. I'm good at dealing with crises. I'm the person everyone runs to for advice, so whatever I find out today, I should be able to deal with it on my own.

I pay the taxi driver, but I don't have the strength to walk through the doors to the clinic, so I collapse on the front step instead. It's like I don't know how to be myself anymore. I last felt like this when my mother left. Just before I started having panic attacks. It's the exact same out-of-control feeling that sent me to therapy for three years, and the thought of going through that again is choking me from the inside out. One minute I want to kill, the next I want to run. And right now, I'm crying, but I want to scream at the top of my lungs because the person I need the most is the only person I can't go to.

It's just after seven thirty and a slow crawl of Wednesday-morning traffic has begun to flow down East 7th Street. Stores opposite me open with a crank and screech of metal shutters, and city workers in smart suits teamed with not-so-smart sneakers head for their offices. An old black guy wearing a beat-up Lakers cap walks past, stops and stares at me. I grit my teeth and look away. He shakes his head, mutters something about "kids" and "drugs" and walks away humming the theme song to *Friends*.

"Can I help you?"

My head snaps around to find a large woman dressed in teal scrubs towering over me. I open my mouth to speak but nothing comes out.

The woman sits down on the step next to me, and all I can think is that I shouldn't be here. "Do you want to come inside?" Her accent has a strong Spanish lilt that accentuates the compassion in her tone. "My name is Rita. I'm a nurse here."

"I need help . . . but . . . I'm sorry. I don't even know if this is where I should be." It would be so easy to clam up and walk away.

Her brown eyes sparkle with kindness. "Help is what we do here." She places her hand on my knee. "And we're unusually quiet this morning, so why don't you come in? I can get you a coffee and we can go from there."

I follow her into the clinic's brightly lit reception

185

area on autopilot, then she takes me into a private room with a desk, a couple of pink chairs and an examination bed. My heart drops a few inches in my chest at how cold and clinical everything seems. You can paint the walls peach, hang up pictures of sunsets, and place as many damn palm plants in the room as you like, but a clinic will always be a clinic. When I sit down, I notice a box of tissues strategically placed on the desk, and I wonder if this room is where well-trained nurses like Rita direct people who come to them swathed in an aura of "victim".

Rita sits down opposite me with a form pinned to a clipboard. "We can fill this in later."

Shit. I didn't even realise. "Um, I don't have insurance. I'll have to pay myself. I only have a credit card, but I'm almost up to my limit, so if I need to pay much—"

"Don't worry about that for now," she says, tilting her head sympathetically. "You're not American, are you?"

"I'm here on a student visa from Denmark."

"Oh, wow. Legoland." Her eyes light up. "I have three boys and a house full of the stuff."

"Yes, it does tend to get everywhere." I return her smile, but I feel too anxious to make small talk with her. My gaze sweeps over my surroundings as an awkward silence fills the room: blood pressure monitors, trolleys stocked with medical equipment, a row of brown wooden cupboards with medical posters taped to them. I need to get this over with. I'm either going to have to talk or walk. Rita doesn't deserve to have her time wasted. "This is hard to explain. I don't know where to start."

186

"Take your time."

I take a deep breath and let the words tumble out. "I'm an actress as well as a student. I walked off the set of a movie I was shooting two days ago. An actor I was working with asked if he could talk to me, so I went back to see him, but when I was alone in my trailer, somebody else came – someone I hate. He brought a bottle of wine. I told him to leave straight away, but he wouldn't go. We argued, then I started to feel sick. I think he put something in my drink. I can't remember anything from last night . . . I mean, I remember some things . . . I know he wasn't alone. They were talking together. I remember there was lots of tugging, and I had this strong feeling that I didn't want them touching me. I just felt so tired. It was like my body was made of iron, but I was so light I was floating. There were flashes too. Really weird, repetitive flashes – just like lightning. I woke up naked and I don't know what happened . . . and I just need to know."

Rita gives me the look I was dreading – pity. "What time did this take place?"

"Yesterday afternoon. Is that too long ago?"

"No, honey," Rita says, shaking her head. "Time is still on our side. Have you showered?"

"No, I was completely out of it for fifteen hours. I came here in a taxi as soon as I could stand up and walk. I still feel really sick and I'm scared. Please just say you believe me."

Her head snaps up. "Of course I believe you," she says, her eyes filling up with enough pity to sink an ocean liner. She opens a drawer, pulls out another form and pins it to her board. But then her expression becomes more serious. "A simple blood

187

test will tell us if there are any narcotics in your system. If there's been rape or any other form of sexual assault, a physical examination will hopefully find evidence."

"Um . . . Okay." My head spins as the words I was trying not to think about tumble freely out of the nurse's mouth. A swell of nausea rises from my stomach and my vision blurs. I force my eyes shut, but it's like the world is spinning off its axis. I feel as though I've spent the entire night throwing alcohol down my neck, and god, how I wish all I had was a hangover.

The next two hours are the longest of my life. The blood test was easy. The recounting of my feeble memories from yesterday was harder. The examination itself was embarrassing, intrusive, distressing. When it's all over, Rita takes me to another room, where I shower, and then she gives me some clean donated clothing – a pair of jeans that are too short and a top with embroidered flowers on the neckline. While I'm waiting for my results, my mind is bombarded with endless questions, doubts and memories. *You don't know for sure. It might all be okay.* I repeat the same line over and over in my head, but I can't convince myself that nothing bad has happened, and I can tell from the way Rita was looking and talking to me that she isn't convinced either. I'm mindlessly flicking through an interior design magazine when she eventually returns.

"So sorry about your wait," she says as she walks back to her chair. There's a clipboard wedged under her arm and she's holding a bundle of pamphlets. She sits down, smiles at me and reaches across the desk to give my hand a squeeze. I wish she wouldn't. I'm desperate for news and I'm trying to read her body language. I can't work out if she's overly gushy, or if she's preparing me to hear the worst. "We found extremely high levels of GHB in your blood."

My eyes fill with tears. "I don't know what that means."

"Gamma hydroxybutyrate. It's a central nervous system depressant used in general anaesthesia and some pharmaceuticals. In small doses, it's used by bodybuilders, and it's common at raves and parties, but it is also used as a date-rape drug. It seems you've been given a very high dosage, which accounts for the time you were immobilised. GHB, at these levels, can act as an extremely powerful sedative."

I choke on a sob as the full horror sinks in. "So, are you telling me I've been raped?"

Rita shakes her head and I welcome the relief that slowly trickles through my veins. "We didn't find any physical evidence of rape, but" – she reaches for my hand again as my mind races with yet more questions – "this doesn't mean you weren't sexually assaulted. In fifty per cent of sexual assault cases, particularly where immobilising drugs have been used, we don't find physical evidence. Your best bet would be to make a full report to law enforcement and have them investigate."

"No," I say, shaking my head. "No, I can't."

"You don't have to make that decision now. You already made a smart move in coming here and getting checked out. We're obliged to keep your medical records on file for a decade, so if you change your mind at any time you can still proceed. Do you have friends or family you could call? Someone who could be here for you? I'd feel a lot better if I weren't sending you home alone."

I think about Nate and I picture his sunshine smile. My heart cracks. "No, there's nobody."

Rita sighs. "Okay, well if you're sure. We don't bill victims of assault, so you don't have to worry about paying for the exam." She passes me the pamphlets. "There's good information here about therapy and reporting crimes of a sexual nature. If you don't want to take this further, please still make sure you get the right help. You may have no obvious physical injuries, but you've still been assaulted."

"Thank you." I glance down at the leaflets. I'm struck by how morose they are. The model – a woman – is gazing sorrowfully through the window of a darkened room. Is that what I look like? "Do you think my memory will return?"

"I don't know, honey," she says.

"Maybe it's a good thing I don't remember."

"My advice would be to get some insurance and get some therapy. But, in the short term, get as much rest as possible. It could take seventy-two hours for the drug to completely leave your system, and even longer for the side-effects to disappear. I suggest you pick up some aspirin for your headache and drop back in to see me tomorrow. Just ask for Nurse Gomez. I'm working the same shift pattern for the next two weeks."

I stand to leave. "Thank you. I'm glad I came."

"I'm glad you came too," she says, walking me

to the door. "Please talk to someone and think hard about reporting this."

"I just want to forget it ever happened."

* * *

I go back home to an empty house and curl up on the sofa with a blanket. I still feel tired, but I can't sleep because my brain won't stop thinking. Every time I close my eyes, my mind takes me back to the bed in my trailer – talking, heaviness, dizziness, the cold, those weird flashing lights. Even though I know I shouldn't block out what happened, that's all I want to do. I want to forget so badly that I'd gladly volunteer for a lobotomy.

After a few hours of restlessness I close the drapes to see if that will help me sleep, but it doesn't. Maybe I slept enough last night. Or maybe I'll never be able to sleep peacefully ever again. Not until I know the truth. And that thought leads me to my next realisation.

I know what I have to do, so I grab my bag and leave.

15

MY LEGS AREN'T SHAKING WHEN I walk into the Beverly Wilshire hotel for the fourth time this week. I don't feel sick and I don't feel scared. The fear that took hold of me this morning, slowly suffocating and then paralysing me, has had long enough to bend me to its will and I'm already tired of feeling like a victim. I'm done losing my mind over what Klein *could* have done to me. I need to know for sure what he *did* do. I've come here for answers and I'm not leaving until I get them. I take the elevator to the floor where Nate's suite is located. He told me that his father always stays in the Presidential Suite when he's in LA, so that's where I go.

Again, my sneakers squeak against the polished wooden floors as I walk past elaborate Roman pillars and ceilings that look like they've been plucked from the Palace of Versailles. A tall floor-standing mirror leans against the wall, and I stop for a moment to check myself over. Same as always, my ten-dollar leggings and oversized slouchy t-shirt don't fit these beautiful surroundings. The thousand-dollar Dolce & Gabbana dress Nate bought me would fit, but the girl who wore that dress isn't me. These leggings are me. I don't want to fit – I never wanted to.

Without thinking, I pull my cardigan up around my neck and fasten the top button. Then I freeze.

Seriously, what the hell am I doing? Is this who I am now? I'm no longer a waitress with an impossible dream or an actress who whips her clothes off for money. I'm a victim. How do I stop behaving like a victim?

I knock three times on the dark oak doors of the Presidential Suite. I hear shuffling from inside, but no voices. The pit in my stomach slumps and my heart starts to race. I inhale a huge lungful of air, then I slowly blow it out.

When the door opens and I'm standing face to face with Lord Klein, his steely grey eyes locked inside a hard expression, I want to turn around and run. Silently, he stands to one side, allowing me to walk into his hotel room. I figure this is either the bravest or the most colossally stupid thing I've ever done.

I spin around when I hear the door close behind me. "Don't lock it."

A sickening grin appears on his face. Klein is in his sixties, his skin dusted with freckles and age spots that dip in and out of creases and sags. He's tall and lean and doesn't look strong, but the way he holds himself – straight shoulders, strong posture, firm jawline – oozes power and influence. "As you wish."

He walks in front of me and stretches out his arm to invite me to sit on one of the plush sofas placed around a glass coffee table in the centre of the living area. "I'll stand, thank you. I won't be here long."

"Suit yourself." Lord Klein sits down on the sofa and crosses his legs. He rolls up the sleeves of his sky-blue dress shirt, then folds his arms in front of him. "Can I get you a drink?"

A drink. He knows exactly what he's just said. His cold stare cracks into an even colder grin that sends a shiver down the full length of my spine. I fight the urge to drive my fist into his face. "Just tell me what you did."

"I did what I had to do. I told you I wasn't going to let you drive a wedge between me and my son."

"That isn't an answer."

"Yes it is," he says bluntly.

I don't understand. Do I have to be more direct? I decide I do. "Did you rape me?"

He lets out a scoffing laugh and shakes his head. "No."

"Did that other guy?"

"No."

I exhale a breath I didn't know I was holding as my aching legs sway underneath me. *Tak gud.* Thank god for that. I fall back against the arm of the adjacent sofa, relief rippling through my body in waves. "Then why did you drug me?"

"I told you already. I did what I had to do." He walks over to a marble-topped console table, puts a key in the front drawer and takes out a brown letter-sized envelope. When he walks back towards me, there's a look of pure triumph on his face. "You *are* very much like Pauline, you know? In fact, I've known many women like you over the years – immoral, duplicitous, untrustworthy – and I've dealt with them all. I wasn't going to let you sink your claws even further into Nathaniel."

My brain can't even process his ridiculous accusations. He hands me the envelope. "What's this?"

"The answers you're looking for."

My hands tremble as I pull out a bundle of photographs. I feel like my heart has stopped beating. A sharp pain lodges in my throat as I stare at the first photograph of me and the stranger who's been haunting my fractured memories. We're lying naked on the bed in my trailer. He has his arms around me and it looks like . . . oh my god. I flick through the rest of the photographs. In one, I'm lying on my back with my legs wrapped around the guy's waist. He has dark hair, steely blue eyes . . . those eyes. I'll never forget his eyes. In another photo we're sleeping, and in another he's. . . he has his hands – hands I don't know – all over me. My stomach lurches at the grotesque images, and the pictures fall onto the floor. This is why he drugged me. So he could do this?

"Don't worry, you weren't harmed."

"You drugged me and you removed my clothes and let that guy touch me and . . . of course I was fucking harmed!"

He looks at me as if I'm crazy. "It was just a mild sedative. Don't be so melodramatic. You've been getting paid to lie naked with strangers, so this wasn't any different."

My breathing becomes tight and painful as my pulse beats harder. I don't even need to ask him how he can compare what he did to me with a choice I freely made to act in a movie.

I stare down at the carpet. The brown, cream and gold pattern blends with the colours in the photograph lying at my feet. My skin, his darker skin, pale-yellow bedding, orange hair, black hair . . . the shapes are blurry, but they clear when I blink away my tears. "Who is the guy?"

"That isn't important."

"It would be important to the police."

He laughs. "Nobody would believe you."

A fire blazes inside me. "Yes, they would. I've been to a clinic and I have a full and very detailed report, including blood test results."

My words reach Klein's eyes instantly. His pupils grow wide and sharp for a moment, but then his natural sneer returns. "GHB is popular with addicts as it provides a very quick and long-lasting high. As I said, nobody would believe that a two-bit waitress and soft-porn actress wasn't also a casual drug user."

"Nate would believe me."

"On balance, he's more likely to believe that the cheap fling he barely knows was sleeping around on him." He laughs. The loud, crackling sound cuts straight through me. "So, now you have a choice to make. Keep seeing my son, and I will show him these photos. Then I will show the press. How would your claims about being drugged go down with your average supermarket tabloid reader? I'm a big name in England, so this would make very interesting reading."

"So would my accusation against you." My voice is shaky and erratic, but I keep battling on.

"Maybe, but not for the reasons you think. A penniless soft-porn actress versus a member of the House of Lords and one of Britain's wealthiest businessmen?"

"You wouldn't risk it . . ."

"Oh, I would. I've risked far more than this with other problems I needed to go away."

"You can't care about Nate. Why wouldn't you

want him to be happy?"

His sneer broadens. "Oh, I do want him to be happy – just not with you because I don't like you. I hated you the second you burst into my meeting and wrecked the business deal I'd spent months working on. Then you drove my son away, and I knew you had to be dealt with. Your actions have led directly to the situation you find yourself in today. Nathaniel is heading back to London on Friday morning, and with you out of the picture, I will get my son back. I don't care what happens to you after that. Spend the rest of your life serving burgers, or become Hollywood's next greatest thing, I don't care. As long as you're far away from my son." He walks towards the door and opens it.

"You haven't won yet," I say. I want to appear stronger, but my voice is weak and my body is trembling.

"Oh, I think I have," he replies with cold indifference.

"Actions have consequences, right?" I say to him. "One day you'll get yours."

I leave the hotel hoping I never have to set foot in the godforsaken place ever again.

* * *

Richie is watching TV when I get back home. The bruises on his face have yellowed and I can finally see his eyes beneath the swelling. He switches the TV off when I sit down on the sofa next to him.

"I tried to call you last night. I was worried."

"I was with some of the guys from the movie.

Sorry, my phone died. I left it upstairs charging."
It's only a half-lie.

"Ah," says Richie, his voice soothing and sympathetic. "I really wanted some expert Freja-advice. I agreed to sell the theatre to the development company. I'm signing the papers with Nate tomorrow."

"What?" My lips thin with rage as my blood pressure starts to rise again. "He promised me. He said he would find another way—"

"No, you don't understand." He takes my hand and rests his other, bandaged arm on his knee, wincing slightly as the weight adjusts. "This is all me. I want to sell up and go back home."

My breath catches in my throat. I can't take any more loss. "Do you mean 'home' as in England?"

He tries to smile, but he grimaces when the movement irritates the scabbed-over cuts on his mouth. "With everything that's happened recently – the stress of not being able to make ends meet, the theatre's demands on my time, not getting any decent acting jobs – I guess I've just had enough. Living out here hasn't worked out the way I hoped. I've got an audition for a British daytime medical soap. It's premiering on BBC2 later in the year. It won't be the same as making it big out here, but at least it's work."

I quickly push away the sadness that creeps under my skin and remind myself that this is about Richie and what's best for his life; it isn't about me. "I understand, Rich." I reach out to gently touch his bruised face. He tilts his head and smiles. "I'll miss you though."

"Why don't you come with me?"

"Um . . . that's a really big decision. I can't—"

"Yeah, you can," he says. He's holding my hand really tight, as if he's trying to hang on to me. "You always make crazy, spur-of-the-moment decisions. It's why we all love you."

He's right, I do. But this time, there's more to consider than throwing myself into an adventure. I want to be with Nate so badly that I would jump on a plane tomorrow. Hell, I'd fly to Antarctica if he were there, but if I had the money to take a hit out on the monster he calls his father, I'd do that too. I know I can't be with him. Not now, not yet and probably not ever. How on earth would we forge a relationship with this hanging over us? I've only known Nate two weeks. I should be able to forget about him.

"What are you thinking?"

I start thinking up excuses. "I don't have the cash for a big move."

"My parents own a couple of flats near London that they rent out. They said I could use one until I get back on my feet. We could still be roomies."

"What about Peyton and Riley? Won't you miss them?"

"They're gone already."

"What? Peyton's gone? Gone where?"

"She's moved back in with her parents. You know her dad's a retired cop, right? He was quite adamant he didn't want his daughter and grandchild in harm's way, living here with me and my beat-up face, so they've gone."

"But they're still around, in the city. I mean, you're practically a father figure to Riley."

"And I'll miss her. I'll miss both of them, but

199

this is about me and my life." He reclines back against the sofa cushions, being careful to support his arm. "What do you always say? You find out who you truly are when you throw yourself into something wild and spontaneous."

I start to laugh, but then all the memories of today and yesterday come rushing at me like they're tied to a speeding train, and laughing just doesn't feel right.

"Hey, what is it?" he asks softly.

"Oh, just some pretty heavy stuff. I've done enough talking about it for today."

"Is it Nate?" he asks.

"Partially."

"If you came to London with me, you'd be able to solve that problem."

"Yeah, maybe." I rest my hand on his knee and give it a little squeeze. "I'm going to bed. It's been a long day."

"It's only seven thirty."

"I'm tired and I have a lot to think about. I do my best thinking when I'm in bed." I stand up, take off my cardigan and toss it onto the armchair. "Can I get you anything before I go up?"

"Nah, I'm good. I've had a tough day with the theatre group today, so I think I'm going to catch an early night myself."

I climb the stairs to my bedroom, close the door and flop onto my bed.

Two weeks. It's only taken two weeks for my life to be completely turned on its head. I tuck my knees up against my chest and unplug my phone from the charger. I expect an avalanche of text messages and missed calls. I unfreeze my home screen and find that I'm not wrong.

Two messages from Katrina, three from Dana, four from JJ, and a frantic text from Richie. I quickly reply to them all before I click on the final message.

NATE: I haven't been able to get you out of my head for a day and a half. God, I miss you so much. I'm so sorry if I upset you. Life is kinda mad right now. I was in meetings all day yesterday, then this Silicon Valley opportunity came up and we had to fly up to San Francisco this morning. I'm landing at LAX around midnight. I want to see you. x

I clutch my phone in my hand and start to sob. I don't know what's killing me more – what happened to me yesterday or having to let Nate go. All I want is to call him and tell him everything and beg him to help me and comfort me and make love to me, but I can't.

So I switch off my phone and do nothing.

16

I WAS SICK IN THE night. The nurse at the clinic said nausea and vomiting were side effects of GHB usage, and boy, was she right. I also slept until eleven a.m.

I shower, dress and go downstairs to find Richie packing up his stuff. I feel a twinge of sadness. Whether I choose to stay here or go to London, I'm going to lose either Richie or JJ.

"Morning, sleepyhead. How are you feeling?"

"Better. It was a rough night. Thanks for sitting with me for a while. I guess I must have eaten something or caught a bug."

He's sorting through a pile of books, arranging them carefully into a plastic box. "Seems you needed to sleep whatever-it-was off."

"I did. I had a really good night once I stopped spewing my guts up. You packing already?"

He registers my surprise with a smile. "Yeah, I'm going to have everything I want to keep freighted over to my parents' house, then I'll probably stick the rest on eBay. If you want anything, let me know."

I raise my hand. "No, you're fine."

"Nate called around."

My stomach cartwheels. "He did?"

"Yeah, a few hours ago. I had to sign all the paperwork for selling the theatre."

"So it's done?" I ask, searching his face to see

how he feels about losing his baby. "Are you okay?"

"I'm relieved." He places a plastic lid on top of the box he's just filled and snaps it shut. "I told him you were sick."

Oh fuck. Like he's going to believe that. "How was he? I mean . . . what did he say?"

"He said he'd call back later." He looks me over as a rigid frown appears above his blackened eyes. "Is everything okay between you two?"

I don't know what to say. So much has happened since I last lay in Nate's arms and told him I'd fallen in love with him. Raw emotions flood my body: hurt, pain, doubt, shame, hate . . . fuck, this is all so unfair. I screw up my face to stop myself collapsing into floods of tears again. Then I force the feelings to the back of my brain. I *will* make them disappear, somehow.

"You're not yourself, Freja. Is it Nate? What's he done?"

"Nothing. It's just . . . he's leaving tomorrow, Richie. I can't put into words how I feel about that. I only met him two weeks ago, so it seems stupid saying this out loud, but I can't bear to lose him."

He stops packing and walks over to me, placing his unbandaged hand on my shoulder. "You know, I've never seen you like this over a guy before."

"Yep. And it sucks. I'm twenty-five, not fifteen."

Richie laughs. "I've never seen Mr Cool like this either."

I subconsciously fold my arms – a classic protective measure which doesn't go unnoticed, judging by Richie's raised eyebrow. I drop my arms to my sides. "Has he said anything?"

203

"He doesn't have to. When I first met him he was dating a girl called Isabella and he was absolutely besotted with her. She was smart and beautiful, and she'd only have to walk into a room for everyone to fall silent and wait for her to speak. She had this aura about her, you know? Pure charisma. But still, Nate never looked at Isabella the way he looks at you."

"We barely know each other." I'm trying to convince myself just as much as I'm trying to convince Richie.

"Why are you so afraid?"

"Afraid?" I breathe out a short puff of air. "I'm never afraid, Rich."

Silence hangs for a moment.

"This time you are."

I fold my arms again. "His dad hates me, we live in different countries, and I'm nothing like the people he mixes with."

Richie's bruised jaw drops. He winces and rubs it. Then he sits down. "Come here," he says, patting the seat next to him.

I do as he asks. "Is this where you give me a pep talk? Isn't that my job?"

"Usually, but today I want to tell you a story about me." I'm intrigued. Richie is a man of few words who always keeps himself to himself. He wriggles around on the sofa, trying to make his strained, beaten body more comfortable. "I told you I moved out here because I wanted to make it big in Hollywood, but I didn't tell you that the small taste of celebrity I had in England had made me an egotistical dick." He sighs deeply and his shoulders slouch. I feel like giving him a hug, but he's still so battered and bruised I'm scared I'd hurt him. "When I joined the cast of *The Rules*, paranormal shows were huge, mainly thanks to *The X-Files*, so I was asked to appear at conventions and talk shows, but I was never really a big name. I caught the tail-end of the show's popularity and got lucky. It was a wild time, but I let my ego run away from me. I turned down a part in a police drama series because it was on a small channel with an unknown cast. That show's still running now."

"Oh. Do you regret that?"

"Yeah, I do. I would have had seven years of good, solid TV work, as opposed to seven years of headaches and disappointments. But, most of all, I regret passing up the role because I'd have been acting alongside Amelia."

"Amelia? As in *your* Amelia?"

"Yeah. She wanted me to stay in England and take the part, but I thought I was destined for much greater things. She supported my decision in the end, but our relationship couldn't survive us being on different continents, in different time zones."

"I already know the chance of me having any kind of relationship with Nate after he goes home is zilch, Richie."

"So don't make staying here the biggest regret of your life." Richie's eyes glisten with grief for the life he's lost, and my heart aches for both of us.

"It's not that simple. I told you—"

"Forget his dad."

If only I could tell him why I can't do that. "It wouldn't work. It's not just one thing, it's—"

"Bullshit. This isn't you. You never look before you leap. You just take a deep breath and head out into the storm."

"And when I do that, life tends to bite me on the ass."

His bruised chin locks hard and he sighs. "Sometimes. But other times it doesn't. There's nothing keeping you here, Freja, and there's a whole wonderful life out there waiting for you to claim it. Don't end up like me – grieving for a path I didn't take and a person I lost because I couldn't accept who I was. I was never going to make it big out here." I open my mouth to protest, but he raises his hand to stop me. "I threw myself into the theatre because I was scared of facing up to the fact I'm not good enough to make it in Hollywood. The theatre became my excuse for continually missing the mark, failing the audition and never getting – and keeping – the girl. I've finally worked out where I should be, but I'm too late for Amelia. She got married three months ago."

"Oh, Richie, I'm so sorry."

He reaches out and places his good hand on my shoulder. "Don't be sorry, be wise. Follow your heart, and fuck all the reasons why you shouldn't, because they're all dumb." He shuffles to the edge of the sofa and puts his hand out for me to help him stand up.

I give Richie a very light hug, then I pick up my phone and message Nate.

I can't let him go home without seeing him, but I have no idea what I'm going to say. I don't want to let him go, and I shouldn't have to, but what would have to happen before I could keep him?

* * *

Nate sends his car, and the chauffeur takes me on a secret mystery ride to Griffith Park. We park under a pink tree against a picture-perfect backdrop of the Hollywood Hills. It's a bright sunny day, and I'm surrounded by children running and laughing, older kids playing soccer and a team of workmen doing something technical-looking with a very large pipe.

Out of the corner of my eye, I see Nate walking towards me. His bronzed skin seems to reflect the sunlight, and his grey t-shirt and black cargo shorts outline his athletic body. He looks so amazing that my breath gets caught in my chest. Or is that achy feeling just heartache? How am I going to let him go when I want to hold onto him with every ounce of strength I have? As I walk to meet him, he tucks his hands into his pockets and dips his head. Then he smiles and I feel like my broken heart is going to shatter into a million shards of knife-sharp glass. I pick up pace, my wedge sandals making me stumble on the dry, grassy earth and my loose plait whipping around my bare shoulders.

We both stand rooted to the spot, neither of us knowing what to say. It's funny how we're both standing on the same patch of grass, under the same blue sky, yet the two paths lit up in front of us are forcing us to take different directions.

"I'm, um, glad you came," he says. His eyes seek out mine. His jaw is tense and his tone is earnest. "I was so worried."

"I'm sorry," I say, wondering how on earth I'm going to explain two days of radio silence without delving into the truth. "I have no words to describe how sorry I am."

"It doesn't matter," he interjects quickly, closing the gap between us. "The only thing that matters is you're here now. I . . ." He digs his hands deeper into his pockets. "I missed you."

"I missed you too."

"You look beautiful."

I feel my cheeks warm up. "Thanks. You don't look too bad yourself."

"Well, you know, a guy has to look his best." His face relaxes and his beautiful all-over-body smile makes a welcome return. My insides start to flutter, but the butterflies are promptly chased away by a huge, aching pit of anxiety infested by grief. "You look great in white. You don't need to wear colour because you *are* colour." His eyes wander over my hair. "I've never loved the colour red as much as I do today."

I let his compliments wash over me. I try to keep it together, but the urge to leap into his arms and start making out with him in full view of the park is overwhelming, so that's exactly what I do. To hell with the world.

The second my lips meet his, he lifts me off my feet and I wrap my arms around his neck. I hear a "Whoop whoop" from the vicinity of the workmen, but I don't care. My hands glide through his hair until I'm cradling the back of his neck, pushing his lips and tongue into my mouth.

After a while, he gently places me back on the ground, but we don't stop kissing. It's as if we're discovering making out for the very first time. I suck on his mouth, tasting every available inch of his sun-drenched skin, but when his hands wander over my body, I flinch. Memories of being held,

208

being touched and being hurt engulf me and I duck out of his hold. "I'm sorry . . . it's just . . . um, we're being watched."

Nate shoots a glare at a sweating, red-faced workman who looks like he's spent the day boiling his head in a pan of oil. The guy whistles and his co-workers erupt in laughter.

"Yeah, maybe we should go somewhere," Nate says with humour, although I can tell he's mildly irritated.

"Here would be fine if it were dark and we were alone."

He quirks an eyebrow. "Really? Now that gives me something to look forward to when you visit me in London. There are dozens of great parks and they're all open at night."

I think of Richie, and London, and how difficult it would be to fire yesterday into outer space on the back of a nuclear missile. Nate's father has laid claim to my happiness, my future and my self-respect. *Why are you letting him take your entire world away from you? Why are you letting him win?*

"What is it?" he asks. I'm about to open my mouth to speak when he leads me over to a little wooden picnic table. There's a wicker basket sitting on top of it. "We may as well talk over lunch."

"Have I found myself in Jellystone National Park? Are there bears hiding in those bushes?"

"Do you mean bears who like to wear green ties and hats by any chance?" He lowers his voice to a whisper. "If so, the park ranger gave me his word that our lunch would be safe from four-legged mammals with a fondness for 'pic-a-nic' baskets."

We sit down next to each other, our hips touching and our legs nudging. The contact still gives me goosebumps, despite the sword of Damocles that is dangling between us. He opens the basket and takes out a bottle of chardonnay, some roast chicken, a tub of potato salad and a small bowl of strawberries. "You still have a thing for strawberries, then?"

He grins and raises his eyebrows. "I've become obsessed with them lately. I even dream about strawberries – or rather I dream about doing things with them."

I pick one out of the bowl and take a bite. "I think you might have made that dream a reality already."

He unscrews the bottle top and pours into two plastic wine glasses. "Doesn't mean I wouldn't want to do it all over again." A light breeze swirls around the picnic area, blowing a loose tendril of hair onto my face. He reaches out and tucks it behind my ears. "I wish I didn't have to leave."

The regret in his voice makes my insides twist. The inability to unburden myself with all my deepest, darkest thoughts and feelings is crushing me. "I wish you didn't too."

He moves one arm around my shoulder and lightly rubs my forearm with his other hand. My head fits into the nook of his neck, and I inhale his cologne while making a frantic promise to myself that I'll never forget how he smells or how he feels.

"So, Richie told me he's moving back to London. He said he'd asked you to go with him. I know it's a huge step, but it would be amazing if you did."

I take hold of his hand. "I'd be lying if I said I hadn't thought about it, but you're right. It *is* a huge step."

"I understand. Being in Hollywood must mean a lot to you."

"To tell you the truth, I'm not so sure about that anymore. I used to love acting, but if I'm only ever cast in roles where I have to take my clothes off, there's going to be a point in time when I'll have to reassess if that's all I want on my résumé. I'm interested in producing, but I don't know if that's right for me either. I need more time before I decide."

"You're Freja. You make spontaneous choices all the time just to see what happens next."

My stomach drags my heart down to my feet. "It isn't that simple."

"I know." His arm moves from my shoulders to my waist. "You have no idea how sorry I am that I have to fly home tomorrow. I know I won't be able to stop thinking about you while I'm gone, and the first chance I get, I'm coming back to see you."

Would that work? If he came back without telling his father every few months? Could we continue seeing each other in secret?

"And if you wake up tomorrow morning and decide to hop on a plane, I will move heaven and earth to get you to London. I'm so excited about the project with Aaron. It's going great already and I have you to thank for that. We have Silicon Valley investors lined up from our meetings yesterday, and I'm confident Wu Chong won't be able to resist investing too. I've worked with Chong before. He's such a smart guy – a real go-getter. Oh, and believe it or not, my dad said he'd like to play a part too."

Mention of his father sends my heart rate soaring. "Your dad?" I lift my head and look straight into his eyes. I feel like he's betraying me, but that's ridiculous. How can I be angry with him when he doesn't know everything his father did?

"I haven't forgiven him for walking onto your set, Freja. I don't know why he did that and it's going to take a hell of a lot of work on his part to make up for all the shitty things he's said and done to you."

I watch his smile fade and his eyes glisten with hurt, but the betrayal is still there – ballooning in my chest, poised to suffocate me. "He hurt me, Nate. He violated my privacy and made me feel dirty and worthless . . . I'm just shocked that you could . . ."

"I don't know if I'll ever stop hating him, or what he did, but . . ." He shrugs and his jaw tenses. "I hate him, but he's still my dad."

All this time I've been worrying that I wouldn't be able to let Nate go, I didn't expect he would say something to make it easier for me. Lord Klein will always be his dad. Nate will always be his son. I can't change those two truths, and any attempt to navigate my way between their relationship would lead to self-destruction. "I hope you'll be able to make things up with your father, Nate, but I never will."

"Freja, look, I know what you're thinking, and I swear I'm thinking it too. I'm not saying I'm anywhere close to forgiving him for barging onto your film set like that. In fact, it makes me want to knock him to the ground, but—"

"I know. He's still your dad." His expression registers my acceptance and he pulls an apologetic half-smile. And this is when I realise I have certainty. I love Nate too much to *not* let him go.

We eat our picnic, we talk more about our hopes and dreams and then, at twilight, we walk up to the Griffith Observatory and gaze at the stars.

"I don't want to go back tonight. I want to spend all night with you."

There's nothing I want more too. One more time – one last time . . . Should I take it, or should I keep the memory of the way things were *before* alive instead? "I think I'd rather say goodbye here in the park with great memories of a lovely day. I don't want you to remember me as a blubbing, emotional mess when you leave for LAX in the middle of the night. It would be too hard."

His sunshine fades to grey. "Goodbye? But . . . you mean 'goodbye for now', don't you?"

The contours of his beautiful face blur into warm, golden shapes, and for once I let my tears fall. "He'll always be your dad, Nate. And you'll always be his son."

"Freja, no, you can't mean . . . I love you. You're the only woman I've ever felt this way about. Please. I don't want to lose you. I need you."

"And I love you too," I say. A sob escapes my throat and my voice cracks. "I have to let you go because I love you."

"But I'll come back . . . I'll come out here every chance I get. Weekends, whole weeks – whatever it takes. Give me a chance to prove how much I love you."

He gently cups my face, his thumb brushing

away my tears. "I already know how much . . . and that is why." His hands freeze, then fall to his sides. He looks like he's been shot in the chest and I hate myself for doing this to him. I hate myself for giving up. But I hate *him*, the creature he has for a father, a hell of a lot more.

"I won't ever forget you," he says.

"Good. I want you to remember me."

Nate takes a taxi back to the Wilshire while his chauffeur returns me to my quiet house. I get a strange sinking feeling when I see Richie's boxes piled high in the living room, alongside trash bags he's filled for the local thrift store. I'm losing Richie as well as Nate, and *he's* responsible for it all – "he" who doesn't even deserve a name. I want to forget about *him*. I want to forget everything – the pain, the shame, the anger – I want it all to go away.

On the way back to my room, I almost trip over something. I switch on the light and smile when I see Riley's Little Mermaid doll. I pick it up. Memories of how excited she was to show me her brand-new favourite princess come flooding back. I'll have to make sure she gets the doll back. Riley believes in mermaids, just like she believed me and Nate – or rather Prince Eric – were destined to be together. I stroke the doll's bright-red hair and reposition her seashell bra top. And then it hits me. I *am* freaking Ariel. And I don't want to stay under the sea. I want to be up there under the sun, with him.

But I can't. Because I don't have legs strong enough to follow him.

He – that creature – has stolen everything that

made me who I am, including my voice, but I *will* get it back. I will break free from this dark undersea cage, then I'll swim to the surface and remember how to dance.

One Year Later

My first day in a fantastic new job, and isn't it just my luck to be running late? I head out of the tube station and instantly curse my decision to wear ridiculously inappropriate-for-absolutely-everything-especially-running high heels.

It's a sunny July day and the London heat is stifling – nowhere near as stifling as a summer's day in Los Angeles, but at least there aren't any mosquitos or killer bees to contend with.

I take off my shoes and run as fast as I can towards Churchill House, a bright and shiny office building in the heart of the Docklands.

My phone buzzes just as I reach the revolving doorway:

RICHIE: Break a leg today, gorgeous xx

I'm just about to text him back when I'm almost knocked to the ground by what can only be described as a whirlwind dressed in my grandmother's dining room curtains.

"Oh my gosh, I am so sorry. How unspeakably clumsy of me! Are you okay?" The woman's accent sounds like it's been plucked straight from a Jane Austen movie. Yes, Freja, you're definitely in England now.

"No harm done," I tell her as her dark, soulful eyes sweep over me. "But it's a good thing I hadn't put my shoes on yet or it might have been a different story."

She looks me over and smiles. Her round face is

warm and friendly, and her chestnut-brown bobbed hair is curled under her chin. "You look lost, sweetie. Where do you need to be?"

"Diablo Brown? I'm actually just starting a new job today."

Her small eyes light up. "I work there too!" She sticks out her hand. "Georgie Ravencroft."

"Freja Larsen," I say, shaking her hand.

"Ooh, your name is beautiful. And you're beautiful. Scandinavian, right? Where are you working? I'm in art. I only started three months ago myself. I came from *Chat* magazine and it was definitely a culture shock for me – in a good way, though. It's really great here. Lucas Bartle – the MD – has such a great vision. Maybe we can have lunch?"

My head spins. Georgie may be the first person I've ever met who doesn't need to breathe when she talks. "Sure. Um, I'm Danish. I'm starting as a junior film producer. Sorry – what else did you ask? I'm running a little late." I pop my heels back on.

"Those are amazing shoes, but how on earth can you walk in them all day?" she says. I eye her clunky wedge sandals and smile inwardly. It seems I've stumbled upon a true English eccentric. Georgie's garish floral dress is a mish-mash of styles from at least three different decades. She must have secured top-secret access to Helena Bonham-Carter's closet. "The film studio is in the basement. I'll walk down with you. Diablo has the best film team in the city. Where were you previously? Somewhere in Denmark?"

"No, Los Angeles, actually."

She takes me through a set of double doors. "Oh

wow, really? What were you doing out there?"

"Acting, waitressing, studying. I completed my master's at UCLA last month, applied for a few junior positions, got on a plane and here I am." She stops dead still. Her hand shoots dramatically to her chest and her mouth falls open. I start to laugh. "What is it?"

"You're an adventurer," she declares with a throaty gasp.

"Well, I guess. Also my American student visa expired."

She flaps her hand dismissively. "Don't spoil it for me. I'm an adventurer too and I've been looking for a soulmate. Why London?"

"No real reason. I have a good friend who lives here with a spare room I can rent."

"Lucky you!"

Of course, I don't tell her I had a very good reason to move to London a year ago, because I never tell anybody that.

Nate kept in touch to begin with: text messages, phone calls, even the odd Skype session. Then, a month down the line, contacted ended. Richie, who was back in London by then, was cut off too. Aaron and JJ last saw him when their tech venture ended in a buyout at the beginning of the year. They told me he was finally setting up on his own and moving out to China with Evelyn. So it seems he did prefer Chanel after all.

I don't blame Nate for cutting ties with me. I know I broke his heart. But it hurts that he cut off his friends. It's true that I let him go. It's also true that I wasn't in a great place to fight for him. My panic attacks and nightmares returned, and the self-loathing, shame and crippling doubt over whether I should have fought harder consumed me. I tried to suffocate the memories by burying them alive in a very dark area of my brain – a place with dragons and monsters and *him*, that creature. But they wouldn't die.

A year later and I finally managed to swim out of my undersea dungeon and get feet capable of walking me into the next chapter of my life.

And so here I am.

Georgie takes me down the flight of stairs to the film studio. Her bouncy personality and quirkiness has instantly won me over, so I enthusiastically accept her kind invitation to have lunch.

"If you need someone to show you around the city, look no further than yours truly. I know all the best bars and – my goodness, I have to tell you – there's this new club that has opened in Mayfair and it's just divine. You have to let me take you. I love looking after new people. Righto, I have to go. I'm on the first floor, in art, by the way. See you at twelve thirty."

My head starts spinning again. I hope Georgie stays away from coffee for the rest of the morning. I dread to think what she's like with a caffeine high. "I'll look forward to it."

She breezes off down the hallway, and I feel a warm buzz creep under my skin. I'm going to go to that club in Mayfair with her. And I'm going to make more new friends. I'm going to excel in my career, and I'm going to sing, and drink, and love and dance. *You made it out the other side, Freja. You're here, and you're alive, and the world is waiting for you.*

For a long time I wanted to forget. Then I wanted to stop feeling angry. The world teaches women that anger is something we should feel ashamed of – that we should strive to overcome it, forgive those who have wronged us and move on with our lives.

I've learned to see things differently. Some things deserve our anger and we have a right to feel it. I want to feel it, because it's real and it's powerful and when I'm ready, anger will be the reason why I will talk.

The End

A MESSAGE FROM GUNTHER
(Max's cat).

If you enjoyed this book, then *purr-lease* would you consider leaving a positive review on Amazon?

Reviews help other readers find Elizabeth's stories and open up different ways of marketing to all the millions of humans out there who will love her books.

She says I (or rather my idiot owner) might get my own story if I can *purr-suade* you. I personally don't know how this will work. Max is a liability. He still hasn't realised that I'm the one who steals the serrano ham out of the fridge. I've been doing it for seven years! Seven!

Mee-ow

When the one who got away returned...

It's been almost eight years since Freja let Nate go. Now she's living in London and has a high-flying career as an advertising film producer. She's older, wiser and setting the world on fire. Is she finally ready to come to terms with her past?

Second Chance – coming soon

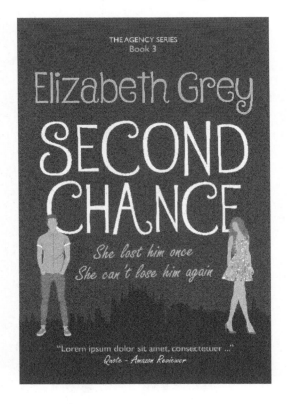

She trusted too much.

A year after Violet graduates from Harvard, she takes a job in New York City. There, she falls into the arms of dashing advertising dynamo, Ryan. But he's keeping a terrible secret that forces Violet into an impossible situation.

WHEN WE WERE YOUNG
Prequels to the Agency Series

Elizabeth Grey

Violet

SHE TRUSTED TOO MUCH

AVAILABLE NOW
The Agency Series
Available to buy now – priced from FREE ☺

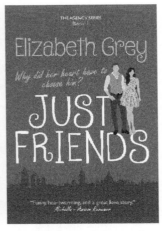

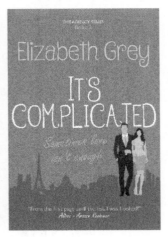

ABOUT THE AUTHOR

Elizabeth Grey spent a sizable chunk of her childhood in North East England locked away in her bedroom creating characters and writing stories. Isn't that how all writers start?

Following a five year university education that combined such wide-ranging subjects as fine art, administration, law, economics, graphic design and French, Elizabeth entered the business world as a marketing assistant before moving into operations management.

Marrying Chris in 2007, Elizabeth now has three young children and runs a small, seasonal business selling imported European children's toys and goods. She is active in local politics and campaigns tirelessly to improve the UK's education system.

During her time as a stay-at-home mum, Elizabeth rekindled her love of writing and thinks herself lucky every day that she is now able to write full time.

When not working, Elizabeth finds herself immersed in her kids' hobbies and has acquired an impressive knowledge of Harry Potter (thanks to the big boy), Star Wars (thanks to the little boy) and Barbie (thanks to her daughter). She loves European road-trips, binge-watching Netflix series and doing whatever she can to fight for a better world.

She's been told she never loses an argument.

Elizabeth's top quotes:

"Real courage is when you know you're licked before you begin, but you begin anyway and see it through no matter what. You rarely win, but sometimes you do." – Harper Lee

"In this life, people will love you and people will hate you and none of that will have anything to do with you." – Abraham Hicks

"Be who you are and say what you feel. Because those who mind don't matter, and those who matter don't mind." – Dr. Seuss

"I am no bird and no net ensnares me. I am a free human being with an independent will." – Charlotte Bronte

"I am not afraid of storms for I am learning how to sail my ship." – Louisa M. Alcott

Printed in Great Britain
by Amazon

44935743R00129